The Collins Book of Stories
for Eight-Year-Olds

D1078629

In the sames series:

The Collins Book of Stories for Four-Year-Olds
The Collins Book of Stories for Five-Year-Olds
The Collins Book of Stories for Six-Year-Olds
The Collins Book of Stories
for Seven-Year-Olds

The Collins Book of Stories for Eight-Year-Olds

Collected by Julia Eccleshare

Illustrated by Jacqui Thomas

Young Lions
An Imprint of HarperCollinsPublishers

First published in Great Britain by
HarperCollins in Young Lions 1992

Young Lions is an imprint of the Children's Division,
part of HarperCollins Publishers Ltd,
77–85 Fulham Palace Road,
Hammersmith, London W6 8JB

ISBN 0 00 674047 2

A CIP record for this book is available
from the British Library

This book is set in Ehrhardt

Printed and bound in Great Britain by
Hartnolls Ltd, Bodmin, Cornwall

Contents

Secrets

Anita Desai

One morning, at school, Rohan got every single sum wrong. Then he dropped a bottle of ink on the floor and it splashed on to his teacher's white canvas shoes. When he made a face behind his teacher's back, he was seen. So he had to be punished.

"Here, take this letter to your father and go home," his teacher said, after writing a long and angry letter. "Let him punish you as well."

Rohan tried to look too proud to care,

and picked up his books and walked out of the school yard and up the narrow city lane. But once he reached the big grey banyan tree that was the only tree in the lane, and found that the cobbler who usually sat under it, mending broken old shoes, was not there, he sat down in its shade, hiding himself in the folds of the great trunk, and sobbed a little with anger. He had not been able to get his sums right although he had tried. He had dropped the ink bottle by accident and not to spoil the teacher's white shoes. Perhaps it was bad of him to pull a face but how could he help it when things were going so badly? Now he was afraid to go home and hand the letter to his father, who would be very angry and beat him. He sometimes did, and often scolded him.

So Rohan hid there in the folds of the grey tree trunk, and poked with a stick at the seeds dropped on the ground by the parrots that ate the red berries of the tree. He was so angry and afraid that he poked and poked with the stick till he had dug quite a deep hole in the dust. In that hole he found a little grey lump of rubber – a plain piece of rubber that some other schoolboy might have dropped there long ago. He picked it up and rolled it about between his fingers.

"I wish it were a magic rubber," he said, sobbing a little. "I would rub out the whole school, like this – like this—" and he stepped out to look down the lane at the boys' school that stood at the end of it, and angrily rubbed at the air with the grey lump of rubber.

Then he stopped, his hand still in mid-air, his mouth still open, and his hair began to stand up on his head as it did on his neighbour's cat's back when she saw his dog.

Something very, very strange had happened. The school had vanished. He had really rubbed it out! The tall, three-storeyed house on its left, with its latticed balconies and green roof was still there, and on the other side the tin-roofed warehouse where timber was stacked stood there too, but in between them, where the school had been, there was now a patch of earth. There was no white school building, no deep verandas, no dusty playground, no high grey wall and not a single schoolboy. There was just a square of bare brown earth between the other buildings, all quiet and still now in the heat of the afternoon.

Rohan's knees were shaking. He ran a little way down the road to see better but still could find nothing but a blank where the school had once been. Then he felt so afraid of the vanished school that he ran back up the lane as fast as he could, snatched up his books and the terrible rubber from among the roots of the banyan, and ran into the road where he lived. He hurried up the stairs at the side of the little yellow house to their room on the roof where his mother hung the clothes to dry and his father stacked old boxes and bicycle tyres.

His mother was alone at home. She was kneading dough in a big brass pan. The fire was not yet lit. "You're early," she said, in surprise. "I haven't any food ready for you yet. But you can go and break up an old box and get me some wood to light the fire. I'll warm some milk for you. Hurry up, don't look so sulky," she said, and began to roll and thump the dough in the pan, roll and thump, roll and thump, so she did not see the face Rohan made as he went out to pull an old crate to pieces and bring in an armload of packing-case wood.

He came in and threw it all into the grate with such force that the ashes and grit flew up and settled on all the pots and pans, and the dough and the neat floor as well.

His mother was so angry, she shouted, "What's the matter with you, you rascal? Look what you've done! What a mess you've made! Now go and fetch the broom and sweep it up at once."

"I won't sweep," he shouted back, as loudly as though there were a devil in him, shouting for him.

She was still more angry. "I won't sweep it up either. Let it lie there and then your father will see it when he comes home," she said.

Then Rohan felt so afraid that he held up the magic rubber and cried, "I won't let you do that. I won't let him see it. I'll – I'll rub you all out," and he swept through the air with the little grey lump of rubber, as hard as he could. He shut his eyes tight because his face was all screwed up with anger, and when he opened them the whole house with the unlit fire, the brass pan, the glass of milk and even his mother had vanished. There was only the roof-top, blazing in the afternoon sun, littered with empty tins and old tyres at the edges but quite, quite bare in the middle.

Now Rohan did not have a home or a mother or even a glass of milk. His mouth hung open, he was so frightened by what he had done. Then he turned and ran down the stairs as fast as he could, so that his father would not come and find him standing alone on the empty roof-top.

He heard an excited bark and saw it was his dog Kalo, who had been sleeping in the shade of an overturned basket in a corner of the roof-top, but had heard him run down the stairs and followed him. Kalo was frightened, too, at the way their room had disappeared and the roof-top left standing empty, so he was running along behind Rohan, barking with fright.

Rohan felt afraid that the people who lived in the yellow house would come out and see what had happened, so he shouted "Go back, Kalo! Go back!" But Kalo ran towards him, his long black ears flapping as he ran. So Rohan rubbed the air with his rubber again and screamed, "I don't want you! Go away!" and Kalo vanished. His round paw marks were still to be seen in the dust of the road. A little trail of dust was still hanging in the hot, still air of that dreadful afternoon, but Kalo the dog had vanished.

And someone had seen. An old man who traded in empty tins and bottles had just started his evening round and, while shouting "Tin and bo—" stopped short and stared till Rohan, rubbing in the air with his rubber again, shouted, "You can't see! You mustn't see!" and rubbed him out. That old man with his grey beard and big sack of clanking tins and bottles just disappeared as Kalo had.

Then Rohan turned and ran even faster. He ran into the big road that went round the mosque. Just in time he remembered that he might meet his father there, for he had a cycle repair shop at the foot of the mosque steps. So he whirled around again. He kept going in circles, as if he were a little mad. At last he ran to the banyan tree, climbed over its roots into a cleft between two folds of the huge trunk and hid there, trembling.

"I'll hide this terrible rubber," he said at last. "I'll put it back in the hole and never, never take it out again." With shaking fingers he scraped more dust from the little hole he had dug earlier, in order to bury the rubber.

As he scraped and dug with trembling fingers, he found something else in the hole. At first he saw only one end of it – it was long and yellow. He dug harder and found it was a pencil. Quite a new pencil – he could see no one had used it before, though it looked old from being buried in the earth. He stopped crying and trembling as he wondered who could have buried a pencil here, and whether it was a magic pencil as the rubber was a magic one. He had to try it and see.

First he dropped the rubber into the hole and covered it up. Then he held up the pencil and pointed it at the bare patch of earth where the school had once stood between the warehouse and the green-roofed house. Very, very carefully he drew a picture of his old white school building in the air. He did it so carefully that he seemed to see the grey lines forming before his eyes. Then he blinked: the grey-white building really *was* there now. Or was it only a picture in his mind? Quickly he drew the verandas, the playground, the high wall, and then the little matchstick figures of a line of schoolboys rushing out of the front gate, the lane filling with them, and saw them leaping and running with their satchels flying behind them.

He stood up and ran a little way down the lane, out of the shade of the mysteriously whispering banyan tree. Now, in the clear sunlight, he could see the school quite plainly again, alive and noisy with children set free from their lessons. He stood there till he saw the teacher come out on his bicycle. Then he turned and ran the other way up the lane.

He stood in the middle of the dusty road and quickly, quickly, drew a picture of a little black dog in the air, as well as he could. He was still working on the long plumed tail when he heard Kalo bark, and saw him bounce down on to the road on his four feet and come pelting towards him.

As he came closer, Rohan saw he had missed out the jagged edge of Kalo's ear where it had been torn in a dogfight. He was careful to add that so Kalo would be exactly as he had been before, scarred and dusty and wild with happiness. Kalo stood still, waiting for him to finish.

When it was done, he shouted "Kalo! Kalo!" and patted him hastily, then went on busily with his pencil, drawing the old, bearded tin-and-bottle man. He was just drawing the big, bulging sack when he heard the cracked voice cry "-o-ttle man!"

and there he was, shuffling down the road and blinking a little in the bright light.

Then Rohan and his dog ran home, up the stairs to the empty roof-top. There, leaning against the low wall, his tongue between his teeth and his eyes narrowed, Rohan drew a picture of his home as well as he could. Even when he could see it quite plainly, the little whitewashed room with its arched windows and pigeon-roost on the flat roof, he went on drawing. He drew a picture of his mother kneading dough in a pan, the fire, the glass of milk and even the broom in the corner of the room. Then he went in and found them all there, just as he had drawn them. But he saw one mistake he had made in his drawing – he had coloured his mother's hair black and left out the grey strands over her ears. She had remained stiff, lifeless. He stood in the doorway, rubbing gently at the unnatural darkness of her hair till it showed the grey he knew. He realized you cannot draw a picture out of desperation, or with careless speed. It took care, attention, time.

When he had finished, his mother moved,

looked up at him. "There's your milk," she said quietly, "drink it up."

He nodded. "I'll sweep up a bit first," he said, and went to fetch the broom. He swept and he swept, enjoying the work that he had not wanted to do at first, till he heard his father arrive, lean his bicycle against the wall and lock it, then come slowly up the stairs.

Rohan ran out, shouting "Look, I found a pencil and a rubber on the road today." He wanted so much to tell his father all about it and ask him how it happened, but he did not dare.

His father was looking tired. "Why don't you sit quietly and draw something?" he said, as he went in for his tea.

Rohan nodded and went to fetch a piece of paper. Then he sat on the top step and spread out the paper and drew. He was not sure if the magic pencil would draw an ordinary picture. It did. Using it very, very carefully now, he drew a picture of Kalo.

When his father saw it, he beamed. He had never seen a picture as good. Rohan showed it to his mother too, and she was so pleased she pinned it on the wall, next to the calendar.

His father said, "I didn't know you could draw so well. Your teacher never told us. You should draw a picture for him."

Rohan spent the whole evening drawing with the magic pencil. He took the drawings to school next day, and his teacher was so pleased with them that he forgot to ask for an answer to his angry letter of the day before. He gave Rohan good paper and time to draw every day.

Rohan drew so much that the magic pencil was soon worn to a stub. Instead of throwing it away like an ordinary pencil, he took it down to the banyan tree and buried it in the earth at its roots where he had hidden the lump of rubber. As he walked away he worried about whether he would be able to draw as well with an ordinary pencil bought at the stationery shop near the school gate. But he had had so much practice now, and become so good an artist, that he found he could do as good a drawing with the new pencil he bought as with the magic one.

He became so famous in that town that people came from miles away to see the pictures his mother pinned to the walls of their house. They went to the school and asked the teacher about him. No one knew how he had learnt to draw and paint so well without any lessons or help. Even when he became a great artist, whose name was known all over the land, Rohan did not tell anyone the story. That was his secret – and the banyan tree's, and they kept it to themselves as secrets should be kept.

Wordfinder

Adèle Geras

I

"It's all very well for you," said Simon's mother, metallic bracelets sliding from her wrist to her elbow as she reached up to fluff out hair which looked to Simon quite fluffed out enough already. "It's me on the sharp end, you know, seeing the teacher and everything. It's me that has to deal with it, while you're sunning yourself by all those Texas swimming pools!" A whining note, thought Simon, has crept into her voice. He lay on the sofa listening to his mother moan-moan-moaning at his father, and imagined all the combined groans, complaints, whinges, reproaches, of all the people on all the phones to America squirming through thick cables lying all over the bed of the Atlantic Ocean, like tiny wriggling snakes, ready to bite, ready to curl into people's ears and make them feel uncomfortable, sad or guilty. OK, so his mother probably had a right to feel a bit peeved. She was stuck here in snow that wasn't even proper snow, but gunge out of the sky which became black slush as it hit the pavement, and Dad was sunning himself in Dallas, probably stretched out on one of those beach chairs, beside a pool with water so blue that it hurt your eyes to look at it. He continued to listen to his mother (yak-yak, clak-clak, and this is costing more than a pound a minute, moan-groan, weep-sigh) even though he know the main theme of her tirade: Simon couldn't spell. Not for toffee. He just had no idea. And the worst of it was, he was not particularly keen to learn. This was what his mum was telling his dad.

"It's not that people aren't trying with him. They are – all the time. I make lists of words till I'm blue in the face, and so does Mr Boyd. Tests him and tests him, and gives him extra time to learn in, and then Simon forgets what he's learnt by the very next day. Mr Boyd says it's like pouring water into a colander. All the knowledge flows out of him as if his head had holes in it . . . well, I am worried . . . he can't go through life like this . . . well, people will think he's stupid and he's not . . . he's intelligent, but he doesn't give himself a chance . . . all his books look as if . . . I don't know . . . as if he's illiterate or something."

Simon pulled a loose thread in his sweater until he'd made a hole big enough for his finger. The truth of the matter was (and he hadn't told a soul this: not his parents, not Mr Boyd, not anyone) he didn't really see what difference it made to anyone, the way things were spelt. If the person reading it knew what you meant, what on earth business of theirs was it if you chose to spell "house" H-O-W-S-E or "table" T-A-B-E-L or "tea" T-I? There were enough things around that you had to keep in your head and get right or else . . . numbers, for instance. Two and two always had to make four. They couldn't make three or five just because you felt like a change. You couldn't meddle with facts. Paris was the capital of France and that was that. You couldn't suddenly decide that today it would be Marseilles and the French could like it or lump it. The distances between places were fixed: Manchester couldn't suddenly edge a hundred miles or so closer to London. But words – that was different. An aeroplane remained exactly what it was, even spelt A-I-R-A-P-L-A-I-N. Simon therefore found it hard that everyone should be so nasty to him about it. The punishments and extra work seemed to him out of all proportion to the gravity of his crime. On the phone, his mother was now sounding a little happier.

"Really? Do you honestly think it'll help?

What did you say it was called? Oh, that's wonderful . . . but I wonder if it'll make any difference . . . gosh, I hope so . . . well, I'll tell you one thing, next time Mr Boyd has to be seen by anyone, it's going to be you. He's more than a little daunting, you know. Sometimes I wonder if he's the right teacher for Simon . . ."

"I wonder that every single day," Simon muttered, "and I know the answer, too. He isn't."

His mother, Simon knew, had happy memories of Miss Gardener, she of the Second Year Infants, who, true to her name, had blossomed in flowery dresses and pink angora cardigans and kissed Simon better whenever he fell over. This paragon spent many happy hours cutting dinky little triangles of green plasticine to stick along the spine of Simon's rather lumpy stegosaurus. She had never burdened her pupils with unwieldy-looking words. Mr Boyd was addicted to proverbs, so Simon reckoned it would be fair to call him a bird of another feather, a horse of a different colour, or even a different kettle of fish. Mr Boyd was thin, tall, grey, pinched, pernickety, bespectacled, leather-elbowed, high-voiced and beaky-nosed, with gooseberry-coloured eyes and no lips to speak of. Sometimes he smiled, showing yellow rectangles of teeth. There was, somewhere, a Mrs Boyd and several small Boyds, but no one in school had ever seen them. Children who could invent monsters, other planets, unseen jungles, witches, wizards and haunted houses dripping blood at the drop of a hat found themselves defeated by the invisible Boyd family, the absolutely unthinkable Boyd household. Simon knew that it wasn't only Mr Boyd's appearance that made him so disliked. Mr Fraser was fat and warty and universally beloved: Mr Biggins was smelly and wimpish but quite nice with it; Mr Fairstone yelled like a sergeant-major, but had a soft heart; Mrs Masters knocked you out with her perfume, but made the most unlikely people skip around the gym like young lambs during her dance classes ... no, Mr Boyd was the sarcastic one, the one with the tongue like a chainsaw. Cut a person to ribbons, he would, just as soon as look at them. My eccentric spelling, Simon thought (OK, let's face it, my downright awful spelling), is just what the doctor ordered for Mr Boyd. Lovely bit of tongue-exercise for him, every day.

"Well now, Simon, Shakespeare says 'question' Q-U-E-S-T-I-O-N. So does Milton. I dare say every author from Chaucer to Enid Blyton says 'Q-U-E-S-T-I-O-N', but not you – oh no. You, of course, are above such mundane considerations as received wisdom. Tell the class, Simon, how *you* have chosen to spell 'question'."

"Mumble . . . mumble . . ."

"I don't think I quite caught that, Simon. A little louder, please. I shouldn't like those at the back to miss such a treasure . . . such a jewel without price."

"Q-W-E-S-C-H-O-N."

(Giggles all round. The gooseberries behind Mr Boyd's glasses ice up.)

And that happens, thought Simon wearily, every day. Every single day.

"Wonderful news, Simon!"

"Off the phone at last? Great. Can we have something to eat now?"

"Yes, of course, but don't you want to hear what your father said?"

"Yeah, OK."

"He's found a kind of spelling game. I mean, a game to help you with your spelling. All the kids over there have it, apparently. It's called 'Wordfinder'."

Simon looked pityingly at his mother. He sighed.

"Terrific. Marvellous. Bloody fantastic. Only a game for babies which we've got over here already. That'll really help a ton. Gee, thanks, Pop!"

"Don't be so ungrateful," said Simon's mother. "I've never seen it over here."

"You've not looked, probably."

"Anyway, I don't care if it *is* for babies, as long as it helps you with your spelling."

The metallic bracelets clinked and rattled

as Simon's mother turned her attention to mashing the potatoes.

II

"If I hear that robot-voice going on and on in that infuriating monotone for one more minute, not to mention that irritating little jingle," said Simon's mother, "I'll kill someone. Probably you."

"You wanted me to practise spelling," Simon said. "You said I should be grateful. You said I should use it more." Simon wondered why it was that so often people got cross with you for doing the very thing they'd wanted you to do. He pressed the "Off" button and looked at his Wordfinder game, still a little surprised that he liked it so much. A little embarrassed, too. It was a toy for kids, there was no doubt about it. Neil's sister Becky had one, and she was five. Simon had made it an absolute condition of his acceptance of the game that no one, not a single one of his friends, should know of its existence. He kept it hidden away in the bottom of his mother's cupboard, the one place in the whole house where his friends would never find it. He would never have admitted it to anyone, but he liked the way it looked: a bright blue plastic case, with all the letters of the alphabet laid out in rows under a small screen. Press letters, and they would appear in lit-up green on the screen, spelling the words that the funny, Dalek-like voice told you to spell. You could choose a program (easy-to-difficult) and if you pressed all the right letters, the robot-voice encouraged you. "Great!" it would say, or "That's the way." If you spelt the word wrongly, the voice didn't hesitate to tell you so, and after two wrong spellings of the same word, it would flash up on the black screen, correctly spelt, to reproach you.

"Now try 'manager'," the voice would say. Or "train" or "story" or "referee". If you misheard something, if the voice was too hollow, too far distant from human speech, there was a neat little button you could press, labelled "Repeat", and then the voice would say the word over and over again. Enough, as Simon's mother put it, to drive a person to drink.

"I don't mind you using it," she said. "I'm delighted when you *do* use it, but I'm watching the news. Can't you see? Why don't you put in that earplug? Then I won't be able to hear a thing."

"I don't like the little plastic thingie in my ear," Simon said, but he plugged it in, just for a bit of peace. He pressed the "Go" button.

"Hi, kid," said a voice that wasn't the robot-voice.

"What? What's happening? Who are you?" Simon said.

"Shut *up*, Simon," said Simon's mother.

"You'd better do like she says, kid, or she's gonna be a mite displeased, I'd say."

"But—"

"You don't have to talk to me, you know," the voice continued. "This here contraption's all fixed up so's I can hear your answer just by being tuned in to your ear."

"That's impossible," Simon thought, making sure to keep his mouth shut.

"Ain't a damn thing that's impossible . . . not nowadays, not with this here technology we got ourselves."

"But who are you?"

"Why, boy, you lost the little bit of sense God gave you? Who do you reckon I am? I'm the teacher."

"Then . . . what's the robot-voice? What's that?"

"That's just a computer-voice. New-fangled machine. That just looks after the game department. You want real teaching, you tune in to me, kid."

"What's your name?"

"My name's Homer Lee Hudson. I guess you can call me Homer Lee. Or HL. I don't mind what you call me. We've got work to do here."

"Hang on a minute," Simon was thinking as hard and as fast as he could. "Are you telling me there's something . . . or, I mean, someone . . . like you in every single Wordfinder game in the world?"

"No, sirree. Teachers ain't exported yet. Don't know of any teachers in any export models of the game. Ain't even in all the US games, not yet. We're only in the Deluxe Model so far, and that's what your dad picked out for you. Right there in Neiman Marcus' store in Dallas, Texas."

"Wow!"

"You said it, kid. Still and all, I don't know why you should think it so strange. Lots of folks who've got the money go hiring tutors and such to help their kids along."

"I suppose so ... but ... well, it's a bit unexpected. That's all. A bit like magic."

Homer Lee chuckled. "Sure is a lot of that about these days, and no mistake. You seen them cameras? You don't have to wait but thirty seconds or so, and there's a picture, bright as flowers, right before your eyes. If that ain't magic, damned if I know what is."

"Mr Hudson?"

"Homer Lee."

"Homer Lee? May I ask you something? Will you tell me what you look like?"

"What do you reckon? Think about me some . . ."

Simon thought. He thought of the lean, elderly, whiskery men he'd seen in films, wearing checked shirts and denim trousers. He thought of leather boots and dusty roads and horses. Homer laughed.

"I guess it's my voice. I guess it's being around cowboys so much, that's what gave you that idea. No, son. I'm old and whiskery all right, but I wear a black suit with a high collar to my shirt, and a tie, and my schoolroom . . . well, you won't see a single book out of place in it, no sir."

"And I bet your children love you, too."

"They'd better . . . or I'll tan their hides." Homer Lee's laugh came at Simon like a song, through the wire.

"You've never so much as raised your voice to anyone, have you?"

"Never needed to," said Homer Lee. "You treat a kid straight and he'll treat you straight. Most times, anyway."

"I wish I could plug you into Mr Boyd's ear for a bit. I wish you could teach him something."

"He don't sound like the kind of person you can teach. The really good teachers, they're the ones who haven't forgotten how to learn. Are you going to be like that?"

"What do you mean? I'm learning all the time. I go to school every day and learn."

"The way I understand it, you like doing your own thing with words. Is that right?"

"I suppose so . . . a bit. I don't see why it's so important."

"Well, why don't you go the whole hog, then? Why bother with 'train' when you could say 'boful'."

"'Train' is easier to say, that's why."

"Just what you're used to, that's all," said Homer Lee.

"But you can't *invent* words. No one else will know what you mean. It'd be another language."

"And you're not doing that. OK. Then let's find some other reasons why you should learn to spell."

"To make my parents happy."

"Can't be bad, but it's not enough."

"To make Mr Boyd happy."

"Don't give a sneeze in a saddlebag about him."

"What then?" Simon couldn't think of one other reason in the world.

"To make sure you don't spend the rest of your days fiddling around with letters of the alphabet and worrying which way round they go, when your mind needs to be taking in ..." (here Homer Lee paused impressively) "... IDEAS. You gotta get over all that nuts-and-bolts stuff and free your head for more important things, son."

"D'you think you can teach me?" Simon wondered.

"I surely do, son, or my name's not Homer Lee Hudson."

"We'll start tomorrow," Simon thought. "My mother's looking at me now. Bye."

"Bye, kid."

Simon pulled the small, white plug out of his ear and blinked.

"You OK?" said Simon's mother. "You've been very quiet for absolutely ages."

"I've been thinking," Simon said.

"Do yourself an injury, all that unaccustomed brainwork."

"I'm putting this thing away now," said Simon and took the Wordfinder box gently upstairs to its place on top of his mother's shoes.

"Good night, Homer Lee," he whispered.

The shiny plastic box was silent. Anyone who heard me, Simon thought, anyone who *knew*, would think I was off my trolley. Homer Lee would call it "crazy" or even "plumb loco".

"Ya-hee!" Simon yelled as he came downstairs. "What've you-all made for supper, Momma?"

His mother was on the phone, and frowned at Simon to shut up. He sat down at the table and waited.

That night, Simon found it difficult to fall asleep. He was racking his brains for some kind of answer. How did they do it? How did they program a computer (because that was what it must be) so that it could read your innermost thoughts and answer sensibly whatever they were? The mind boggled and continued boggling. Perhaps there were similar games for every subject, all sold under different names, with all kinds of computerised physics teachers, maths teachers and zillions of foreign language teachers shut up in boxes ready to be plugged into ears. But if that were so, then why wasn't more fuss made about it? Why wasn't the "teacher" prominently advertised, or mentioned in the leaflet that came in the box . . . perhaps it was. Simon could hear the television burbling quietly to his parents in the lounge, so he crept out of bed and across the landing to their bedroom. He took the Wordfinder leaflet out of the box and read it in the light shining in from the landing. "At last," it said, "your own computerised spelling teacher!" In large letters all across the front. But that could be the robot voice. There was nothing about . . . wait . . . what was this? Could it be? Simon read, right at the end of the leaflet: "For more private learning-to-spell fun, use the earplug provided."

That must be it. Still, it didn't convey anything quite like Homer Lee. Simon couldn't get rid of the idea, stupid though he knew it to be, that the elderly teacher was somehow real, and had been very conveniently shrunk and packaged in this shiny plastic case. Maybe, Simon thought, I've imagined the whole thing. I'd better check. He fumbled in the box, looking for the plug, fitting it into the "Wordfinder".

"Are you there, Homer Lee?" he thought, and listened. He could hear nothing but a regular and wheezy snoring. Simon smiled and pulled out the earplug, marvelling at the ingenuity of the Wordfinder programmers. He shut his mother's cupboard and tiptoed back to bed.

III

"I have to concede," said Mr Boyd, handing Simon's composition back to him, "that over the last six months your spelling has vastly improved. Yes. That I do have to concede. It is no longer the work of a drunken spider and for this we must, I suppose, all give thanks. However," and he looked at Simon out of chilly gooseberry eyes, "you have lately developed a distressingly American turn of phrase, to say nothing of horrors such as 'color' and 'theater' and the like. Painful turns of phrase and words such as 'elevator', 'sidewalk' and 'pocket book' are as common in your work as raisins in a scone." Mr Boyd permitted himself the luxury of a little half-smile at the felicity of this image. "I shall have to start penalising you, Simon, if you persist in this vein. I give you fair warning. Never let it be said that one of my pupils expressed himself in a manner reminiscent of J. R. Ewing." He smiled another smile, this time congratulating himself on his up-to-dateness in knowing of the existence of J. R. Ewing.

Simon looked down at his desk. He'd hardly heard a word that Mr Boyd had been saying, not properly. He was worried about

Homer Lee. For the last couple of days, the old teacher had been slow to answer. His voice had begun to slur and thicken. Simon knew this was probably because the battery needed replacing, but it was hard to escape the hollow, painful feeling that Homer Lee was dying. Simon shook his head to dispel such thoughts. It'd be all right. Dad had said it would. He was taking the Wordfinder into the shop this morning. Right at this very moment, most likely, he was asking for a new battery. Homer Lee would be restored. All would be well.

"'Fraid you'll have to do without your Wordfinder for a bit, old boy," Simon's dad said at supper, and Simon paused with his fork halfway to his mouth. "Chap at the shop said they'd have to send the thing back to the States. Don't have the facilities over here for your model, it seems. The Deluxe. Still, it'll only take six weeks, he said. Very good after-sales service, he said. Sorry, Simon. I suppose I should have waited and bought the English version but your mother got me all in a tizz."

"It's OK," said Simon. "I'll wait."

He ate silently, thinking of Homer Lee in the blue plastic case, thinking of a whiskery old man laid out in a coffin. Damn it, it was a computer. Homer Lee wasn't real. And couldn't, therefore, be dead. Simon knew all this, knew also, that all it needed was a bit of twiddling and fiddling with micro-chips and suchlike, and Homer Lee would be good as new. But I'll miss him for the next six weeks, Simon thought. He was like a private friend, all the more precious because no one else knew about him.

"I hope," said Simon's mother, "that they get a move on. That machine's done wonders for Simon's spelling. I never would have thought it could have such an effect. And I hardly ever hear that irritating jingle nowadays. Why do you always plug it in, Simon?"

"I don't like the jingle either," Simon said, and sighed. Six weeks! Where was Homer Lee now? In the belly of some jumbo jet, probably, out over the Atlantic. Come back, Homer Lee, Simon thought, squeezing his eyes tight shut, beaming the thought from his mind as powerfully as he knew how . . . come back quickly . . . come back.

IV

Simon shut his bedroom door. His hands trembled as he took the Wordfinder out of its box. It had arrived hours ago, just as he was leaving for school, and he'd had to endure hours and hours of suspense, sitting there, just knowing that Homer Lee was waiting for him at home. He hadn't been able to concentrate. Several teachers (though not Mr Boyd) had asked him kindly if he felt quite well. Now here he was, just about to say . . . to think.

"Homer Lee? Are you there, Homer Lee?"

"Why, good evening, young man," said a woman's soft voice. "I don't know who Homer Lee is, I'm sure, but you can call me Miss Emily. I can sense you're confused, child, but don't you fret now. I'm your new teacher and I'm sure we're going to get along just fine."

"Homer Lee was my teacher. He was the

teacher in this box. I'm used to Homer Lee. What happened to him?"

"He was my predecessor, is that right? Well, I guess he must have moved on. Teachers do, you know ... move on or fade away." She laughed, a tinkling silvery laugh. "I'm so sorry, dear. But if he was such a fine teacher, why, I'm sure he'd like to think of you going on with your studies. Wouldn't you say so?"

"I suppose so. But I shall miss him. I'd got used to him. Will you teach me spelling?"

"Certainly. I'm sure we'll get on splendidly if we work hard together. Tell me a little about ... about my predecessor."

Simon thought hard about Homer Lee, about what he looked like. If this computer is so clever, let's see what it makes of memories and imaginings.

"Why," said Miss Emily, "he seems like a fine old gentleman, if a little rough and ready in his speech patterns. I think we should try for a little more refinement of expression, don't you?"

"I suppose so," said Simon, wondering

what Mr Boyd would say if he found "refinement of expression" in one of Simon's compositions. Have fifty fits and take all the credit, most likely.

"You seem to be an intelligent child," said Miss Emily. "I'm sure you'll do well."

"But I can't picture you at all. Tell me what you're like."

"Well, I have on a mauve dress with a lace collar and my hair is dark. I wear it in a bun at the back."

"Thank you," thought Simon. "I have to go and do my homework now."

"I'll see you again tomorrow," Miss Emily said. "Don't forget to bring a clean handkerchief. I like each child to have one, every day. Those who don't . . . well, at my last school, I made them stay in during recess and stitch one out of cotton from the sewing box." Simon listened to her silver laugh.

"Bye, Miss Emily," he thought, and took the plug out of the Wordfinder, and the small plastic earpiece out of his ear. She can't make me make hankies during recess

... I suppose she means break. What a lot of nonsense! She's only a voice. She's not real. And if these programmers are so clever, why couldn't they put Homer Lee back? They're trying too hard, that's what. Trying to make their "school" like the real world, where you just get to like a teacher, and then either you move up, or they leave ... It's a mistake ... computer teachers should be there for ever, or what's the good of them? Hemming hankies at break! Where has she been? Hasn't she heard of tissues? Simon pulled a face at the Wordfinder box. Poor old Miss Emily. She wasn't a bad old stick, but Simon knew with a certainty that filled his head with sadness like a cloud, that there'd never be another Homer Lee. Real or not, Simon mourned his loss.

"I'll miss you, Homer Lee," he said aloud, glancing back at the Wordfinder to make sure the earplug was safely out of the socket, and Miss Emily couldn't hear. She was, after all, his new teacher, and Simon had no wish to hurt her feelings.

The Slave
who became Chief

Charles Mungoshi

Kakore was Chief Chisvo's slave. When still a boy he was captured after a battle in which most of his own people were killed by Chief Chisvo's army. Now he was a full-grown man and he lived in the Chief's guta, herding hundreds of cattle and goats.

Kakore was above the age when most men had wives and children of their own because nobody would offer their daughter to a slave. At first he had thought about escape, but he knew that the Chief's young warriors would soon recapture him. Also, if he did escape, he wouldn't know where to go once he left the guta. He would die of hunger or he might be eaten by the wild beasts living in the thick jungle nearby. Kakore didn't know where any of his people who had survived the battle lived. As he had grown up, his memories slowly faded and now, as a young man, he couldn't clearly remember his mother and father. This made him very sad.

Chief Chisvo was not hard on Kakore, yet he rarely saw him in his everyday life as a herdsman. But the young men of the village, and even some of the children, never let a day go by without reminding him that he was a slave. They made it clear through their words and actions that they could do whatever they liked with him. His life was in their hands. He was not even allowed to look at any of the girls in the guta. The price of being a slave was to live alone without a wife, cook his own food, fetch his own water and firewood, and wash his own clothes.

Kakore lived in a hut near Chief Chisvo's

cattle pens. His only companions were his dog, his mbira and the single spear with which he hunted hares and rabbits for his meals. In the evenings, when he had corralled the Chief's cattle and goats, he would sit in his hut playing his mbira and singing the rainmaking songs of his now distant land. The animals were his only audience. They would look at him with their sad eyes and listen to him as they chewed.

But one year a severe drought struck Chief Chisvo's land. First, the wells dried up, then the little streams, then the big rivers and finally the deep hippo and crocodile pools. Then, in the second rainless year, even the trees failed to bring forth new spring leaves. Rocks and boulders in the nearby hills split and set fire to the mountains. The wild game, on which people lived, left the land to search for greener pastures. The only food available was lean meat from the cattle that were dying in their hundreds. But there was still a little water high up in the granite hills where it oozed out in thin rusty trickles from ancient rocks. It took the most agile young warriors and girls a whole day's journey to collect, and people feared that even this little water would soon dry up.

Chief Chisvo's people were, therefore, most surprised to learn that, whenever Kakore came back from the pastures in the evening, he carried a goatskin bag full of cool clear mountain water. This was discovered by some young boys who helped Kakore corral the Chief's cattle and goats. Kakore heard them complaining how thirsty they were and gave them some water from his bag. He told the boys to promise not to tell anyone. But who keeps a slave's word? So the boys had gone home and told their elders who, in turn, told the Chief.

Now Chief Chisvo was an old man and very wise. He told his people to leave the slave alone. If it was the slave's wish that no one should know where he got his drinking water, then the Chief would not interfere with his wish. He said he had experienced calamities worse than hunger befalling whole villages because of foolhardy people who did not respect the customs of others.

But only Chief Chisvo and some of his elders and seasoned warriors had such wisdom. The hot-blooded young men, who had not yet been to battle, knew of nothing that was sacred to a slave. Why, they thought, should he have fresh water to drink in their own land when they did not?

So a few young men of the guta – including some of Chief Chisvo's sons – got together to plan how to make Kakore show them where he had found water. Some suggested that they tie him up and then force him, at the point of a spear, to tell them his secret. But the older ones among them said that if they did this Kakore might prefer to die and then where would they be? After all, they argued, Kakore was a slave, they his enemies, so he might happily go to his death knowing that everyone in the guta would die of thirst and, in this way, his people would be avenged. No, older young men advised, the best plan would be to follow Kakore when he took the animals out to pasture and watch everything he did.

"What happens if he has magic that tells him he's being followed and decides not to go to the water?" some of the more impatient young men asked.

"In that case," the older ones replied, "we will watch him day and night. Sooner or later he will feel that he needs a drink. That will be our moment." The young men had thought this was a slow way of doing things but they had been taught not to argue with people older than themselves.

As it turned out, it wasn't at all difficult to find out where Kakore got his water from. In fact, Kakore himself seemed not to care whether or not anyone saw him performing his magic. He just drove the cattle and goats straight up into the hills playing his mbira, his dog snapping at the heels of the animals. Once up in the hills, he went a little higher and sat down on a flat rock from where he could watch the grazing animals and have a view of the guta. The young men following Kakore, hiding behind a large boulder, had the biggest surprise of their lives. They saw that he was sitting on a rock but it was the huge musasa tree against which he was leaning that finally drew their attention. The tree seemed to grow straight out of the middle of the rock and it had the greenest leaves they had ever seen. Every other blade of grass, every shrub and bush and tree in the whole land was tinder dry, yet here was a huge tree in full bloom! There were even rain-birds singing and twittering in its thick foliage!

The young men's previous courage deserted them. They felt they were in the presence of a power much stronger than themselves, or their Chief or the strongest of the Chief's n'angas. The way the slave sat leaning against the tree as if he owned it! Not only that, but the way he moved his head, scanning the lands below him as if everything were in his hands.

The young men felt helpless watching Kakore, as if they were in the grip of a supernatural power. They couldn't retreat because they felt that the slightest noise

would reach the ears of the man under the tree. They weren't even sure whether he was a man or an ancestral spirit. So they stayed rooted behind the boulder, breathing very lightly, as they were afraid that Kakore might hear them.

Then they heard strains of the most haunting mbira music in the world. It was as if the earth had opened and released all its spirits to roam the land freely. The young men trembled. They knew, without doubt, that they were witnessing something not meant for them or perhaps for any living being on earth.

Then they realized that Kakore had begun to sing. It wasn't really singing but the kind of noise one would expect to hear from a big tree as its roots are torn out of the ground. Yet they could hear the words clearly,

"I call upon you, Little Cloud
Swirl and swell, Little Cloud
Twirl and spin, Little Cloud
Let go, Little Cloud, let drop
Let drop a little dew."

Then it seemed as if the sky shattered and a forked tongue of the whitest flame sprang out of the rock. The whole mountain seemed to explode in a deafening roar which faded over the distant land. Then there was a grumbling as if a lion were behind the next boulder. Suddenly the young men felt heavy blows clubbing their heads and, before they realized that it was raining, they were soaked to the marrow. They didn't even wait to see what happened next. They didn't even discuss whether they should go back home. They were already in their mother's huts, behind bolted doors, when they remembered that the rain had stopped immediately, as soon as they left the hill. The land was as dry as ever before. They felt very ashamed that they had left their spears and clubs and bows and arrows on the hill but they also knew that nothing could persuade them to go back and fetch them.

Back on the hill, when Kakore saw that there was enough water to fill his bag from the hole in the rock at the foot of the tree, he began to chant another song,

"Old Chief Sun
Old Chief, hear me
Come out, Old Chief
Burn down, burn all dry
Come now, Old Chief Sun."

And the sun came out in all its fierceness and drank up every little drop of water that had fallen in the most hidden and sheltered nooks and crannies.

For three days the young men who had followed Kakore up the mountain would not talk, even among themselves, of what they had seen. It seemed as if a strange sickness gripped them. They would neither eat nor speak when spoken to. Their people could not understand what had happened to them. They went to consult the most powerful n'anga of the guta but he couldn't understand what had come over the young men. All he could say was, "They must have seen death."

Every day Kakore took the animals into the hills and brought them down again in the evening carrying his goatskin bag of cool clear water and playing his mbira, seemingly unaware of what had happened in the guta.

Then, early one morning, just before sunrise, Kakore received some very important visitors in his hut, Chief Chisvo himself and his eldest advisors. After they had exchanged greetings, the Chief, without wasting time, said simply, "Help us" and looked at his advisors as if to confirm that he had said the right words. The elders nodded their heads in unison and Kakore understood what they meant.

He took down his goatskin bag from a peg above his stool and had a little drink without saying a word to his visitors. Then he held out the bag and the Chief who received it took a little drink of water. (How he would have loved to take a longer and deeper drink!) In silence the bag was passed to everyone in the room and they all took a sip of cool clear water. When everyone had drunk a little, the bag returned to its owner, the slave.

Kakore now spoke softly and with great

sadness. "In my land, among my people, it is the custom to give our visitors a drink of water before any conversation, even before any greetings are made. You may have come a long way without water, and what kind of person would I be if I engaged you in useless talk when you might be drawing your last thirsty breath?" The Chief and his elders nodded their understanding. Then, without another word, Kakore stood up, took his mbira and began to play as he led his guests up the hill . . .

What else is there to say? The moment the Chief and his elders stepped down from the shelter of the big musasa tree they were immediately soaked to the skin.

Back in the guta, Chief Chisvo called a meeting with his advisors, army generals, n'angas and Big Aunts of the Land. No one said anything after the Chief had said what he had to say.

The preparations for the installation of the new Chief were made in a very wet two weeks. It was that kind of quiet but persistent rain that soaks deep into the heart of the earth without turning the top soil into a rock-hard corn-thrashing floor. There was no lightning or thunder but a quiet downpour, soothing to the ear and echoed by the sound of the birds in the hills and crickets and frogs in the flooded plains and overflowing rivers.

In the third week, when the sun came out of the clouds, Chief Chisvo handed over his instruments of chieftainship to Kakore, the former slave and rainmaker. And, since it was the custom of that land that no one should rule the people without a wife, Chief Chisvo himself asked one of his eldest unmarried daughters if she would "help the new Chief run the affairs of the guta".

The feast of the instalment of the new Chief lasted for a whole month. No one, not even the eldest of the elders of the guta, could remember a feast that had lasted so long. But the real surprise was revealed in a remark that one of the Chief's youngest sons made to his father afterwards, "There was so much drinking over so many days and yet not even Musindo and Chikukwa picked a quarrel." He was a hot-tempered young man who had just graduated from herding goats, and there was nothing he liked better than an exchange of blows. He hoped that he would see lots of blood during the feast and felt disappointed that not even the most querulous drunks of the village – Musindo and Chikukwa – had taken advantage of the feast to entertain him to a fist fight.

It was said that in the years that Kakore ruled in Chief Chisvo's land there was never a war. Even more surprisingly, Kakore never seemed to give orders, yet things were always done and he is the best-remembered Chief that ever ruled the land. When Kakore died, he was buried under the musasa tree on the hill and that is where the people go to pray for rain, even today, whenever there is a need.

Cheating

Susan Shreve

I cheated on a unit test in maths this morning during the second period with Mr Burke. Afterwards, I was too sick to eat lunch just thinking about it.

I came straight home from school, went to my room, and lay on the floor trying to decide whether it would be better to run away from home now or after supper. Mostly I wished I was dead.

It wasn't even an accident that I cheated. Yesterday Mr Burke announced there'd be a unit test and anyone who didn't pass would have to come to school on Saturday, most particularly me, since I didn't pass the last unit test. He said that right out in front of everyone as usual. You can imagine how much I like Mr Burke.

But I did plan to study just to prove to him that I'm pretty clever – which I am mostly – except in maths, which I'd be okay in if I'd memorize my times tables. Anyway, I got my desk ready to study on since it was stacked with about two million things. Just when I was ready to work, Nicho came into my room with our new rabbit and it jumped on my desk and knocked the flash cards all over the floor.

I yelled for my mother to come and help me pick them up, but Carlotta was crying as usual and Mother said I was old enough to help myself and a bunch of other stuff like that which mothers like to say. My mother's one of those people who tells you everything you've done wrong for thirty years like you do it every day. It drives me crazy.

Anyway, Nicho and I took the rabbit

outside, but then Philip came to my room and also Marty from next door, and before long it was dinner. After dinner my father said I could watch a special on television if I'd done all my homework.

Of course I said I had.

That was the beginning. I felt terrible telling my father a lie about the homework so I couldn't even enjoy the special. I think he knew I was lying and was so disappointed he couldn't talk about it.

Not much is important in our family. Marty's mother wants him to look okay all the time and my friend Nathan has to do well at school and Andy has so many rules he must go crazy just trying to remember them. My parents don't bother making up a lot of rules. But we do have to tell the truth – even if it's bad, which it usually is. You can imagine how I didn't really enjoy the special.

It was nine o'clock when I got up to my room and that was too late to study for the unit test so I lay in my bed with the light off and decided what I would do the next day when I was in Mr B's maths class not knowing the eight- and nine-times tables.

So, you see, the cheating was planned after all.

But at night, thinking about Mr B – who could scare just about anybody I know, even my father – it seemed perfectly sensible to cheat. It didn't even seem bad when I thought of my parents' big thing about telling the truth.

I'd go into class jolly as usual, acting like things were going just great, and no one, not even Mr B, would suspect the truth. I'd sit down next to Stanley Plummer – he is so clever at maths it makes you sick – and from time to time, I'd glance over at his paper to copy the answers. It would be a cinch. In fact, every test before, I had to try hard not to see his answers because our desks are practically on top of each other.

And that's exactly what I did this morning. It was a cinch. Everything was okay except that my stomach was upside down and I wanted to die.

The fact is, I couldn't believe what I'd

done in cold blood. I began to wonder about myself – really wonder – things like whether I would steal from shops or hurt someone on purpose or do some other terrible thing I couldn't even imagine. I began to wonder whether I was just bad to the core.

I've never been a wonderful kid that everybody in the world loves and thinks is great, like Nicho. I have a bad temper and I like to have my own way and I argue a lot. Sometimes I can be mean. But most of the time I've thought of myself as a pretty decent kid. Mostly I work hard, I stick up for little kids, and I tell the truth. Mostly I like myself fine – except I wish I were better at basketball.

Now all of a sudden I've turned into this criminal. It's hard to believe I'm just a boy. And all because of one stupid maths test.

Lying on the floor of my room, I begin to think that probably I've been bad all along. It just took this maths test to clinch it. I'll probably never tell the truth again.

I tell my mother I'm ill when she calls me to come down for dinner. She doesn't believe me, but puts me to bed anyhow. I lie there in the early winter darkness, wondering what terrible thing I'll be doing next, when my father comes in and sits down on my bed.

"What's the matter?" he asks.

"I've got a stomach ache," I say. Luckily, it's too dark to see his face.

"Is that all?"

"Yeah."

"Mummy says you've been in your room since school."

"I was sick there, too," I say.

"She thinks something happened today and you're upset."

That's the thing that really drives me crazy about my mother. She knows things sitting inside my head the same as if I was turned inside out.

"Well," my father says. I can tell he doesn't believe me.

"My stomach *is* feeling sort of upset," I hedge.

"Okay," he says and he pats my leg and gets up.

Just as he shuts the door to my room I call out to him in a voice I don't even recognize as my own that I'm going to have to run away.

"How come?" he calls back, not surprised or anything.

So I tell him I cheated in the maths test. To tell the truth, I'm surprised at myself. I didn't plan to tell him anything.

He doesn't say anything at first and that just about kills me. I'd be fine if he'd spank me or something. To say nothing can drive a person crazy.

And then he says I'll have to call Mr Burke.

It's not what *I* had in mind.

"Now?" I ask, surprised.

"Now," he says. He turns on the light and pulls off my covers.

"I'm not going to," I say.

But I do it. I call Mr Burke, probably waking him up, and I tell him exactly what happened, even that I decided to cheat the night before the test. He says I'll come in on Saturday to take another test, which is

71

okay with me, and I thank him a lot for being so understanding. He's not friendly but he's not absolutely mean either.

"Today I thought I was turning into a criminal," I tell my father when he turns out my light.

Sometimes my father kisses me goodnight and sometimes he doesn't. I never know. But tonight he does.

The Old Stone Faces

ANN PILLING

Every day, on his way to school, Joe Parker walked with his mother past the old stone faces.

The Parkers lived in a small flat over the tuck-shop in Holywell Street, where Joe's mum was kept busy all day, selling newspapers and sweets and tobacco to all the people who walked up and down that dark, twisty street, one of the oldest and most mysterious in the whole of Oxford. It is a city full of the most fascinating and curious things, but nothing fascinated Joe Parker more than the old stone faces stuck up above some railings round an ancient yellowy-stone building in Broad Street.

There were seventeen of them, all in a row, and each one was different. Seventeen massive stone heads, with stone hair and stone beards, staring out across the traffic at the students going in and out of Blackwell's bookshop. Some of the faces were sad and bored-looking, others were grumpy. Joe's favourite was old Goggle-Eyes who looked as if he'd just seen a ghost. But though they were all different, the seventeen faces had one thing in common – they all looked extremely miserable, and Joe felt sorry for them.

"Come on, Joe," his mum said one day when they were rushing to school as usual. "Staring at those funny old statues again! Do hurry up, or we'll be late."

"Who put them there, Mum?" Joe asked as they went along. "What are they for? And why do they look so fed-up?"

Mrs Parker wasn't really listening. Her head was full of the things she had to do when she got back to the sweetshop. There was the new paper boy to talk to, and the ice-cream people to phone, and the old professor's special tobacco to order from the suppliers.

"There must be *somebody* who could tell me about them, Mum," Joe was saying. "Surely *somebody* must know."

It was his mother's turn to stop in the middle of the street. She'd had an idea.

"There is, Joe. I've just thought of the very person. Why don't you ask Professor Owen Morgan Jones? He's sure to know. They say he's the oldest professor in Oxford. He'll be in to collect his special tobacco on Friday. You could ask him then."

"I *will*," said Joe.

But when Friday came the rain was pouring down, and Holywell Street was as black as night.

"Joe," Mrs Parker said. "Put your anorak

on, will you, and pop down to Number Thirty with Professor Jones's tobacco."

Two minutes later Joe was knocking on the professor's door.

"Come in, Joe," said a whispery old Welsh voice. "Come in and get warm, it's a nasty old day."

Soon Joe was sitting by a roaring fire with a mug of hot cocoa and some ginger biscuits.

"My mum sent you the special tobacco," he said. "And ... and ..." Then he stopped. He felt rather frightened of Professor Owen Morgan Jones. There was something mysterious about him. His small sharp eyes were such a bright green, and his beard was the whitest and bushiest Joe had ever seen. He looked centuries old.

"You've got something to ask me, haven't you?" the Professor said, opening the tobacco and filling his pipe.

"How do you know?" Joe asked in surprise.

The old man laughed. "You don't live as long as I have, Joe, if you don't keep your wits about you, and your ears open. I'm the oldest professor in Oxford, you know. Well, what's your question?"

"It's about those statues in Broad Street, the big stone heads on top of the railings. What are they there for? And why do they look so unhappy?"

Professor Owen Morgan Jones puffed on his pipe.

"People have argued about those heads for years and years, Joe, and none of them knows the true story. Some say they're great Roman emperors, or old Greek poets. Others say they might be advertisements for various kinds of beard – you'll have noticed that all their beards are different, I suppose?"

"I have," Joe said. "But that doesn't explain why they all look so miserable."

Suddenly the professor clutched at his sleeve in excitement. "*That*," he cried, "is the most important question of all! Clever boy to have asked such a question! The fact is, Joe, that those stone heads are not kings or poets or advertisements at all. Those are the heads of nothing less than the *Pontybodkin Male Voice Choir*."

"The *what?*" Joe said.

"The Pontybodkin Male Voice Choir!" Professor Jones repeated. "One of the most wonderful choirs in Wales. Many years ago they came here and gave a special concert at the Town Hall. It was a marvellous concert, Joe, the whole of Oxford came to listen to them, the tickets were sold out months ahead. But when it was over, and they were going back to Pontybodkin, something terrible happened."

"What?" Joe whispered.

"A spell was cast upon them, by the Witches of Wellington Square."

When he heard this Joe nearly jumped out of his skin. "Are there really witches in Wellington Square?" he stammered. "That's the way I go to school. We walk through there every day, me and my mum."

Professor Jones took his hand and squeezed it.

"It's all right, Joe, they left Oxford years ago."

"Why?"

"Well, nobody liked them very much, and *they* didn't like the climate. They complained that it was too foggy and damp. So they emigrated. But the night of the concert – you do know that witches can't sing, I suppose?"

"No I didn't," Joe said.

"Well, they can't. Anyway, on the night of the concert they sat outside the Town Hall, blocking the pavement with their broomsticks, howling jealously in chorus while the glorious singing was going on inside. Nobody listened to them, of course, and a policeman moved them on in the end. But what do you think they did?"

Joe shook his head.

"They glided off down the Banbury Road and hid themselves in some big trees, waiting for the Pontybodkin Male Voice Choir to drive past on its way home. It was a cold rainy night, very like this one, and the coach driver didn't look back till he was well on the road to Wales. But after a few miles he turned round and said, "Well, lads, it was a right royal performance tonight. How about a few songs for me?" And do you know what, Joe? That coach was completely empty and all that was left of the Pontybodkin Male Voice Choir was a row of stone heads in Broad Street."

There was silence in the small, dark room, and Joe listened to the rain clattering against the window. Professor Owen Morgan Jones stared into the fire sadly.

"Such singing, Joe. So beautiful. It would almost break your heart. I should like to hear it just once more, before I die. Will you help me?"

Without waiting for Joe's answer the old man had climbed onto a stool and was lifting an enormous book down from a shelf. He spread it open on his knees and began to look through it. At last he stopped, and read down a page carefully.

"Here it is, Joe. Here we have it. This tells us how to—"

"To bring back the Pontybodkin Male Voice Choir?" Joe interrupted in excitement.

"Not quite, Joe. You see, they've been up

on those railings a bit too long really, and when the Witches of Wellington Square emigrated they crossed the sea – and that always strengthens their kind of magic. But at least this book tells us how to make the heads sing again. I'll need your help though."

"But, Professor Jones," Joe said, "why don't you make them sing yourself?"

"I'm too old, Joe," he said wistfully. "The book says that what must be done can only be done by a small boy, someone about your age. How old are you?"

"Seven and a half," Joe said nervously.

"That's perfect then. Will you do it?"

"Well, I'll have a go," said Joe.

A few minutes later it was all arranged. Professor Jones copied something down from the old book, folded the piece of paper, and pushed it into Joe's hand.

"Take it home, Joe, keep it safe. Don't read it yet, but when the time comes, take it with you."

"But how will I know *when* the time has come?" Joe asked, feeling rather bewildered.

"To release the Pontybodkin Male Voice Choir," Professor Jones said triumphantly, "three things are required: a clear moonlit night, a pure black cat, and the words you've just put into your pocket. A moonlit night's no problem, though we may have to wait a bit. You've not got a pure black cat I suppose?"

"I'm afraid not," Joe said.

"Don't worry. One'll turn up eventually, it always does. Now off you go. Your mother'll be wondering what's happened to you."

The squally weather lasted for ages. Joe didn't bother to check on the clear moonlit night because he knew there must be thick clouds all over the sky, and in any case the pure black cat hadn't shown up yet.

There were hundreds of cats in Oxford, tabby and tawny, marmalade and grey, black cats with white paws, white cats with black paws, cats that slipped out from alley-ways and rubbed against his legs, cats that peered down at him from crumbling old walls. Once, in the pet shop, Joe thought they'd found the cat they needed, but when it was lifted out of the window he spotted three white hairs under its chin, and he turned away in disappointment.

"I'm sorry," he said to the lady. "But you see, it has to be pure black."

Then, one night, when he was asleep, bright moonlight shone into his eyes and woke him up. He got out of bed and tiptoed across to the window to look out. The night was thick with stars, and the most brilliant moon Joe had ever seen was floating across the sky. *It was time.*

Quickly he felt under his mattress for Professor Jones's piece of paper. Then he crept downstairs, through the shop, and stepped outside into the cold crisp night.

Seconds later he was standing in Broad Street in front of the railings, staring up at the big carved faces. The dead stone eyes stared back at him coldly, and the stone beards twinkled with frost.

Joe looked down and saw a tiny black cat sitting on the pavement, its face raised to his expectantly. Its tail was curved like a question mark as if to say, "I'm ready, Joe. Are you?"

"What do we do first, I wonder?" Joe said aloud, and at once the little cat took a flying leap upwards and landed neatly on the great stone head at the end of the row.

It stayed there for a minute, peeping down through the carved stone curls, dabbing at the long stone nose with its paws, then it leaped onto the next head, and the next, until every one of those seventeen statues had felt the warm, soft paws of the furry little cat on its icy-cold face.

As the cat leapt from head to head something amazing happened. The faces came to life. One wrinkled its nose and sneezed loudly, another yawned and cleared its throat, a third shook its head violently and opened and shut its mouth several times. Then they all peered round at each other curiously and when they saw their friends were awake too their big stone faces were wreathed in smiles.

But none of them spoke. They were all nodding and winking at each other silently,

and looking up at the stars, as if to say, "It's a fine night, mates!"

Suddenly, Joe remembered the piece of paper. He unfolded it carefully and read it through under a street lamp, then he spoke the simple words aloud, in a firm clear voice:

> *"Stone men of Wales,*
> *Silent so long,*
> *Awake! And thrill this city*
> *With your song!"*

And as the last words of the spell echoed along Broad Street the seventeen men of the Pontybodkin Male Voice Choir opened their mouths, and sang.

Miraculous singing it was, as rich and as mellow as ripe fruit. The great sound rose up and floated out over the frosty rooftops as Joe stood by the railings with the black cat purring in his arms, his whole body tingling as he listened to the most wonderful music he had ever heard.

They warmed up with a few short songs

in Welsh, and with *Land of My Fathers* and *Men of Harlech*. Then, after a pause for a bit of coughing and clearing of throats, they burst into a great hymn:

> *"Guide me, O thou great Jehovah,*
> *Pilgrim through this barren land!"*

All along Holywell Street doors were opening, sash windows were being pushed up, heads were popping out. From Catte Street and Ship Street, from George Street and St Giles, people were coming to hear the strange singing, for the miracle of the music had woven itself into their dreams.

In no time at all Broad Street was filled with people in pyjamas, yawning students and landladies in flowery dressing-gowns, all bleary-eyed and happy as they listened, and the Pontybodkin Male Voice Choir sang on and on, making up for all its years of silence with marvellous song, as the clocks of the city crept steadily on towards midnight.

"They'll do *requests!*" the crowds whispered to each other in excitement. "Let's see if they'll sing something for us. Let's ask for the old favourites. Go on, you ask them . . . no, *you* ask them . . ."

And they sang a Latin school-song for two rumple-headed students in yellow pyjamas:

"Gaudeamus igitur Iuvenes dum sumus!"

they bellowed joyfully. And they sang *"Pack up your troubles in your old kitbag"* for the park keeper who'd once been a soldier. And for Mrs Mutton, the old widow-lady who lived next door to Joe, they sang a quiet verse of *"God be with you till we meet again"*, and when they sang this the tears rolled down their stone cheeks, and splashed on to the pavement.

Suddenly, high up on a tower, a church clock rang out. It was a quarter to twelve. The choir finished Mrs Mutton's request and fell silent. A shiver went through the crowd and people muttered "Don't pack it up yet, lads. Give us another song!" And the cry was taken up on all sides. "More! More! We want more!"

"Silence, all of you!" a stern Welsh voice shouted from somewhere at the back. "There is one more song to come. Silence, and you will hear." And then the Pontybodkin Male Voice Choir broke into the mightiest song of all:

"Hallelujah! Hallelujah!
For the Lord God Omnipotent reigneth!"

The little black cat had jumped out of Joe's arms and was lost in the crowd. He felt cold suddenly, but then a warm hand was slipped into his. It was the professor.

"Thank you, Joe," he said. "You did it. I knew you would."

"And He shall reign for ever and ever!
Hallelujah!"

the choir sang out. Professor Owen Morgan Jones stood there listening, with the little boy at his side. And the glory of it filled the city.

Joe felt terribly sleepy next day as he hurried along Broad Street, at the last minute as usual. His mum didn't know what a late night they'd had, he and the professor. She slept at the back of their flat, and she hadn't heard a thing.

When he looked across the road at the heads Joe half-expected them to have disappeared. But they were there all right, all seventeen of them, and he did think they looked just a little less miserable than usual.

Fishing with Dicky

Sally Christie

Last summer, my brother, Dicky, got a fishing rod. He fished all through the holidays and I fished with him. I fished with my net, though sometimes Dicky let me hold the rod. I caught tiddlers in the shallows; Dicky caught dace and roach and – once – a trout.

When the holidays were over, Dicky went to his new school.

I'm still at Tidshore Primary. I'm younger than Dicky, see.

*   *   *

"More peas?" said Mum.

I shook my head and covered my plate with my hands. I love frozen peas when they're frozen but they're boring when they're cooked.

"Manners," said Mum. "*No, thank you.* Dicky?"

"No, thanks," he said.

"It'll have to be you then, Phil. All right?"

"I won't say no," said Dad, making room on his plate.

Mum got up and went to the cooker. "Two fish fingers left," she announced. "Any takers?"

"Me!" I shouted.

"Pre-packed, over-priced rubbish," said Dad.

"I've got to go," said Dicky.

It was always like that when we had fish fingers now. Sooner or later Dad would make a pointed remark and Dicky would leave. You see, Dad had loved it over the summer, when Dicky had brought home fish from the river, and he couldn't get used to things having changed. When Dicky and I had come home with the trout, and Mum had cooked it with butter and almonds, Dad had opened a bottle of wine. He and Mum had clinked glasses and Dad had said, "Here's to our fisherman! Long may he fish! Who needs fish fingers when we've got Dicky!"

"Give over, Dad," Dicky had said, but he'd smiled.

To me, the best thing about that trout had been the almonds. I never liked eating the fish Dicky caught. I felt sorry for their poor, cooked heads and their dried-up eyes; I choked on their bones; and – when Mum told me to stop holding my nose – all I could taste was river.

Give me fish fingers any day! I thought as Mum delivered one of the two from the cooker to my plate. But I missed not going fishing with Dicky any more. It wasn't as if *he'd* stopped going: just that things had changed.

Dicky was already up, shoving his chair

under the table, taking his plate to the sink.

"Fishing?" said Dad, as if he didn't know.

"Yep," said Dicky.

"Good luck!" said Dad, as if he really thought there was some point in saying it.

Dicky slammed the door and was gone.

"Oh dear," sighed Mum. "I wish you wouldn't go upsetting him like that, Phil."

"*Me* upsetting *him!*" said Dad. "What about the other way round? If he's so sensitive about fish fingers, why doesn't he bring us some of the real thing? I don't know what's come over him, I really don't. There's something going on."

I folded up the crispy, golden coating of my last fish finger, which I'd carefully peeled off and saved, and popped it into my mouth with a big "Ahhh!" Mum looked at me and winked.

"*We* know why Dicky's not catching anything these days, don't we?" she said. "He's not taking his lucky charm – his lucky

Charlie – that's why not!" (No, I'm not a boy, in case you're wondering. Charlie's short for Charlotte.)

"And that's another thing," said Dad.

"Now, Phil," said Mum. "We've been through all this before. New school – new friends. It's nice for him to be in with a group. Of course they don't want little sisters around. And how much fish they catch is their business."

Dad just grunted.

"What's for afters?" I said.

I'm not like Dad. If I were, I'd have asked, "Can I come?" every time Dicky picked up his rod. But I knew what the answer would have been, so I didn't. I didn't think I'd be fishing with Dicky ever again. But there I was wrong.

Two days after the day of that fish finger tea, Dad's aged aunt died. The funeral was to be on Saturday, and Mum and Dad were both going. They'd be away the whole day, because Great Aunt Anne had lived a long way off: it would take them hours and hours to get there, and hours and hours to get back.

"So, Dicky," said Mum, "you'll have to look after Charlie. Gran can't come over because she's going to the funeral too, and Charlie can't go next door because next door are away."

"Can't I go round Susan's?" I said quickly. I didn't want to hear Dicky saying he didn't want me.

"Sorry," said Mum. "I spoke to Susan's mum at the school gates this morning: Susan's with her dad this weekend."

I shot a glance at Dicky. He looked furious. Then,

"Why me?" he burst out.

"I've just told you, silly," said Mum. "There's no one else. Anyway, you can have a good time together. I'll give you money for the pictures, if you like."

"Yeah!" I said. "Let's go to the pictures, Dicky!" Everything was going to be all right, after all. But,

"I'm going fishing," said Dicky.

"Then you take Charlie with you," said

Mum. She was getting impatient. Dad was washing up, and I knew she wanted to get back to the kitchen to check he wasn't using the scratchy wire thing on the plates.

"She'll fall in the river," said Dicky.

"I won't!" I said.

"Oh, for goodness sake, Dicky, *of course* she won't," said Mum. "How many times have you fished together before? And how many times has Charlie fallen in? So don't give me *that*. If you've a *real* reason – and I don't expect to be told what it is – then you can just give fishing a miss for once. Go to the pictures instead. All I'm saying is, wherever you go, Charlie goes too."

"I'm going fishing," said Dicky.

"Fine," said Mum, and dived into the kitchen.

"Oh gawd," said Dicky.

"I don't want to go stupid fishing, anyway," I said.

"Oh *gawd*," said Dicky.

I'd meant it when I'd said that I didn't want to go fishing, but as Saturday came closer

I got more and more excited. I couldn't
help it: I remembered those days in the
summer when Dicky and I had sat on
the river bank side by side, Dicky's float
bobbing mid-stream, my net lurking in the
water just beyond our toes. A minnow would
dart in; I wouldn't dare move. "Dicky," I'd
whisper. "Look." Dicky doesn't move either,
but he sees.

"Steady, Charlie, bring it up slowly."

My hands tighten on the handle of the net
and I start easing it upwards, pushing against
the current, wondering when the minnow
will realise what's going on. The minnow
darts again, but not quite out. "Steady,
steady," breathes Dicky. And then my net
breaks the surface of the water and I yell
and there's a tiny sliver of silver flipping
around inside, on the green plastic mesh.

Before I learnt to listen to Dicky, I always
yanked the net up as soon as I saw a
fish swim in. And the fish was always
quicker than me. "They always will be,"
said Dicky. "You have to get them with
skill, not speed."

Skill, not speed – skill, not speed I chanted to myself, going to bed on Friday night. And I didn't count sheep when I couldn't get to sleep: I counted little, darting fishes – into my net.

Next morning, Mum and Dad left early. Mum had made two boxes of sandwiches for Dicky and me to take with us for lunch: they were there on the table when I came into the kitchen with my net. Dicky was in there too, fiddling about with his open-face fixed-spool reel. It looked like the body of a tiny, shiny motorbike, and Dicky was always doing things to it, like a motorbike mechanic making adjustments to his machine.

I picked up one of the sandwich boxes.

"I'm ready," I said.

Dicky glanced up. "You're not having that."

"Oh, sorry," I said. "Didn't know they were different." I put the box back on the table and picked up the other one. Maybe Mum had made Dicky egg mayonnaise, which were his favourite. Maybe mine were peanut butter and banana.

Dicky glanced up again. "No, *that*." He meant my net.

"But we're going fishing," I said, "aren't we?"

"*I'm* going fishing."

"But Mum said . . ."

"*I'm* going fishing, you're tagging along. You're coming with me but you're not going to fish."

We had a really big argument then. Dicky said his friends wouldn't want someone poking about in the water with a kiddy's seaside toy. This was serious fishing, he said. I said, if it was so serious, how come he never caught any fish? I reckoned he didn't want me to take my net because he was afraid I'd catch a tiddler – and that would be more than he'd done in the last three weeks!

We went on and on, round and round, until Dicky suddenly looked at his watch. "Now I'm going to be late," he said. "You coming or not?"

As I stomped past him through the back door, he snatched the net from my hand. I made a horrible face but said nothing.

That September was very mild. It was like summer slowly fading, not winter coming on. Cycling along behind Dicky – cycling as fast as I could, to keep up – the wind rushed fresh but not cold in my face. It blew away my rage about the net. I began to feel excited again.

"Dicky!" I shouted. "Slow down!"

It didn't really matter that he was drawing further and further ahead because I knew the way to the river perfectly. But I wanted to let him know that I was speaking to him again.

"Dick–y!"

I thought he was going to ignore me, till I heard him jam on his brakes. And then he didn't just slow down: he stopped. I came up beside him, puffing and laughing.

"Dicky, I . . ."

"Another thing you've got to get into your head," he said. "From now on, I'm not Dicky. I'm Rich."

Still I puffed, but I stopped laughing. I was puzzled. I stared into Dicky's face.

"*Rich*," he said. "OK?"

"But Dicky's your name and . . ."

"Richard's my real name. And now I want you to call me Rich."

"But you're not Rich, you're Dicky!"

"I'm *Rich*!" he shouted, and thudded my handlebar with his fist. "Dicky's a stupid name. I'll chuck you in the river if you call me it today. Rich, Rich, Rich! It's important."

He got back on his bike and set off again. I followed. I was a little scared now. Not scared of Dicky, but scared because now I knew he was.

He was out of sight by the time I turned off the road down the Petherton bridleway, but when I reached the farm track that led to the river, he was waiting for me. The track was too rough to ride along, so we got off our bikes and pushed them. We'd always done that, but in the old days we used to talk as we went.

There were two boys on the bank when we

arrived. Two boys, two bikes, two boxes of sandwiches. The boys looked about Dicky's age, though one was quite a lot bigger than him.

Two boys, two bikes, two sandwich boxes. But only one rod. The smaller of the boys wasn't fishing but just sitting, stirring their tinful of maggots with his finger.

"Wotcha," said Dicky.

"You're late," said Big Boy.

"Hey, Rich, that a new kind of maggot you've got?" said Maggot Boy.

"Sorry, Max," said Dicky, looking at Big Boy. "She's my sister. Got to look after her today. Couldn't get out of it."

"When you come in with us," said Max, "that doesn't mean you get a family pass." He swore. "You'll be bringing your granny along tomorrow!"

Maggot Boy laughed as if that were the best thing he'd heard all year.

"Shut yer gob!" said Max, and to Dicky: "Oh, forget it. Tell her to play with her dolls or something – over by the fence."

The fence he meant was a line of posts

and rails separating the river bank from a great grassy field. There were cows in the field, distant blobs of black and white.

"Get over by the fence," muttered Dicky, and I went.

I like cows, actually. I like their big dark eyes and the way they'll wrap their tongues round a tussock of grass and tug. I liked the idea of the cows in that field much more than I liked Dicky's friends. So I turned my back on the river and began picking grass to offer to the cows.

It was quite a while before I'd got a bunch that I thought would be enough to attract their attention. When I had, I climbed on to the fence and waved it above my head.

"MOOOOO!" I shouted.

The cows took no notice, but someone behind me swore.

"Tell her to shut her gob," came Max's voice.

"Shut up, Charlotte," said Dicky.

I was so surprised to hear him call me that – no one ever calls me that – that I swivelled round on the fence. And what I *saw* surprised me even more. I let my bunch of grass fall to the ground. Now I knew why Dicky didn't catch anything these days. The answer was simple – though I couldn't understand it.

Dicky didn't fish.

Max fished and now Maggot Boy fished – using Max's rod. (It had what looked like an old kite reel tied on to the handle with shoe-lace.) Dicky's rod – the rod that Uncle Ed had given him for his birthday – Dicky's rod with its beautiful, shiny, open-face fixed-spool reel – was in Max's fat red hands.

Dicky sat by Max, watching Max's float. Nobody spoke.

And then Max's float twitched. Straight off, Dicky said, "Steady, steady." I wondered how long it had taken Max to learn to listen to Dicky's advice.

Well, Dicky talked Max through the catch, and Max, like a robot, did what Dicky said, and soon there was a biggish fish – a roach, I think – dangling over the water, on the end of Max's line.

"*YES!*" yelled Max, as if he were punching the air with the word.

"Max-a-*million*!" said Maggot Boy.

Dicky just reached out and quietly unhooked the roach.

The fish he used to catch in the old days he'd knocked on the head at once. He said it was painless to kill them that way, and the sooner you did it, the kinder it was. I'd always thrown back my minnows, except once when I'd sneaked one home in a jam jar – and Dicky had been furious then. "You're cruel," he'd said. "A fish like that needs running water." And sure enough, by the time we'd set out for the river again, the minnow was dead.

But here was Max telling Dicky not to kill the roach, and here was Dicky emptying sandwiches from one of our boxes and filling the box with water and slipping the live roach in.

"I'll see to him when we're done," said Max. Then Maggot Boy passed him a maggot and he hooked it and cast his line again.

I couldn't understand it. I crept forward to look at the roach in the box. It lay straight and still, like a silver spearhead. Its nose was pressed into one corner, its tail splayed out against another. Some crumbs from our sandwiches floated above its head.

I felt more sorry for this fish, with its sleek reddish fins and pumping gills, than I'd ever felt for the fish Mum cooked till their fins were charred and their eyes dull and crinkly. "Poor thing," I whispered, and reached out to stroke it.

I don't know whether I'd even touched it, when the body suddenly flexed and thrashed.

SSHLOCK! The sides of the sandwich box jolted, and for an instant the water churned. Then, while water still splattered on the ground round about, the fish was a silver spearhead again.

I was so surprised, I just crouched there and stared.

"Oi!" said Max, half-turning. "Get her away from that!"

Dicky shuffled round on his bottom and ordered me back to the fence.

"And she'd better stay there," said Maggot Boy. "Tormenting helpless creatures. It's cruel."

Back by the fence, I stuck out my tongue at him, but he was prodding maggots in the tin, and didn't see. I think he preferred prodding maggots to fishing.

The cows had moved closer, but only by chance, it seemed. I sat down on the ground with my back against a fence post. In front of me, the boys sat in a line on the bank; half-way between us sat the box with the fish in it.

I felt cross with myself for having tried to stroke the roach. How stupid that had been! Just because the roach was there, imprisoned in the sandwich box, I'd thought that that had made it suddenly tame. Stupid, stupid, stupid. I'd thought . . . But then I realised that I hadn't thought at all.

I was feeling crosser and crosser, wanting to kick myself or pull my own hair – when something really weird happened.

Somebody else pulled it for me, from behind. Not just pulled, either: tugged, dragged and went on dragging.

"*DICKY!*" I screeched, as I was hauled to my feet.

Heading backwards through the fence, I twisted round and saw – a cow!

For a moment I looked into her big dark eyes; knew (though couldn't see) that she'd wrapped her tongue round my pony tail. And then Dicky was there, clapping his hands and shouting, "SHOOO!" And the cow let go.

My scalp felt as though I'd been dragged twice round the world, though actually I hadn't even gone right through to the field. I clutched my head.

"You all right?" said Dicky.

I nodded. I saw that in the field *all* the cows had gathered to stare. They must have come up behind me while I sat against the fence post. It was surprising to think how quiet they must have been.

"They're just inquisitive," said Dicky. "They don't mean any harm."

I tried to spot the one who'd been most inquisitive of all: she seemed to have melted back into the herd.

"Mooo?" I said to the line of black and white faces, but none of them replied.

And then, from behind us: "Dicky."

We turned.

"Dick, for short," put in Maggot Boy. "Or Sick." He sniggered.

"*Dicky*," Max said again.

Dicky said nothing and nor did I.

"You never said your name was Dicky," Max said. "You should've. It's a good name: good for *you*."

When Max wasn't speaking it seemed very quiet. Still, too. Nobody moved – except, now, Max, who laid down Dicky's rod and stood up.

"*Why* didn't you say your name was Dicky? Shy, were you? Tell you what, come here and whisper the reason now."

Dicky moved forward. I knew he was dead scared. Beside him, I went forward, too. I knew all this was my fault.

I had to step over the roach in the

sandwich box. There it lay, waiting. Not helpless and tame, I knew now.

We stood before Max. I pressed close against Dicky. Max kept his eyes on Dicky. "Get her away," he said – meaning me. "Little girlies should play with their dolls."

But Dicky said nothing. He was too scared to speak. The only sound at that moment was the quiet, quiet ripple, from behind Max, of the river. Max reached out to shove me aside. The river whispered. I don't know whether he'd even touched me, when suddenly I pushed him in.

He looked surprised. As he toppled, arms flailing, he looked at me and he looked *surprised*. Then he hit the water.

After that, there was lots of noise. Splashing, of course, and shouting and swearing. Max had got tangled with Maggot Boy's line, and Maggot Boy was trying to reel it in; Max was shrieking that the hook was in his bum, and Maggot Boy was cackling that they'd catch a whale with that. The river was deep and quite reedy where Max was, but he was lunging his way to the bank. The bank

was steep just there, with no foot-holds, but Maggot Boy would soon pull him out.

And then we'd be for it.

"Quick, Charlie," Dicky yelled. "Run!" He snatched up his rod and made for our bikes.

I started to run and then stopped. Turned back. Max hadn't yet reached the bank.

I ran to the sandwich box. Picked it up – carefully, steadily – in both hands. Max thrust his hand towards Maggot Boy's outstretched one, but the two didn't touch: Max still wasn't quite close enough.

"Steady, steady," I told myself. I felt the roach shudder. *Don't start thrashing, please.* And I raised up the box like some trophy I'd won. Steadily, up above my head. And then flung it.

Over the heads of the boys. To the river.

SSHLOCK! One thrash and, in mid-air, the plastic prison was flicked away. For a moment a spearhead hung in the sky, then the fish was dropping, flexing wildly, falling back to the water.

"Charlie!" screamed Dicky. "Come *on*!" Max had got to the bank.

I ran.

Pushing our bikes up the rough farm track – pounding into pot-holes, rattling over ruts – I thought mine was going to buck out of my hands. Or fall to pieces. But it did neither. Dicky kept beside me – though he could have gone much faster.

We came to the bridleway, mounted our bikes. Still Dicky didn't pull ahead.

We came to the road, looked left, looked right.

Looked back. No one in sight.

Dicky laughed.

And I knew he'd never go there again.

There were plenty of other places to fish.

Children of Wax

Alexander McCall Smith

Not far from the hills of the Matopos there lived a family whose children were made out of wax. The mother and the father in this family were exactly the same as everyone else, but for some reason their children had turned out to be made of wax. At first this caused them great sorrow, and they wondered who had put such a spell on them, but later they became quite accustomed to this state of affairs and grew to love their children dearly.

It was easy for the parents to love the wax children. While other children might fight among themselves or forget to do their duty, wax children were always well-behaved and never fought with one another. They were also hard workers, one wax child being able to do the work of at least two ordinary children.

The only real problem which the wax children gave was that people had to avoid making fires too close to them, and of course they also had to work only at night. If they worked during the day, when the sun was hot, wax children would melt.

To keep them out of the sun, their father made the wax children a dark hut that had no windows. During the day no rays of the sun could penetrate into the gloom of this hut, and so the wax children were quite safe. Then, when the sun had gone down, the children would come out of their dark hut and begin their work. They tended the crops and watched over the cattle, just as ordinary children did during the daytime.

There was one wax child, Ngwabi, who

used to talk about what it was like during the day.

"We can never know what the world is like," he said to his brothers and sisters. "When we come out of our hut everything is quite dark and we see so little."

Ngwabi's brothers and sisters knew that what he said was right, but they accepted they would never know what the world looked like. There were other things that they had which the other children did not have, and they contented themselves with these. They knew, for instance, that other children felt pain: wax children never experienced pain, and for this they were grateful.

But poor Ngwabi still longed to see the world. In his dreams he saw the hills in the distance and watched the clouds that brought rain. He saw paths that led this way and that through the bush, and he longed to be able to follow them. But that was something that a wax child could never do, as it was far too dangerous to follow such paths in the night-time.

As he grew older, this desire of Ngwabi's to see what the world was really like when the sun was up grew stronger and stronger. At last he was unable to contain it any more and he ran out of the hut one day when the sun was riding high in the sky and all about there was light and more light. The other children screamed, and some of them tried to grab at him as he left the hut, but they failed to stop their brother and he was gone.

Of course he could not last long in such heat. The sun burned down on Ngwabi and before he had taken more than a few steps he felt all the strength drain from his limbs. Crying out to his brothers and sisters, he fell to the ground and was soon nothing more than a pool of wax in the dust. Inside the hut, afraid to leave its darkness, the other wax children wept for their melted brother.

When night came, the children left their hut and went to the spot where Ngwabi had fallen. Picking up the wax, they went to a special place they knew and there Ngwabi's eldest sister made the wax into a bird. It was

a bird with great wings, and for feathers they put a covering of leaves from the trees that grew there. These leaves would protect the wax from the sun so that it would not melt when it became day.

After they had finished their task, they told their parents what had happened. The man and woman wept, and each of them kissed the wax model of a bird. Then they set it upon a rock that stood before the wax children's hut.

The wax children did not work that night. At dawn they were all in their hut, peering through a small crack that there was in the wall. As the light came up over the hills, it made the wax bird seem pink with fire. Then, as the sun itself rose over the fields, the great bird which they had made suddenly moved its wings and launched itself into the air. Soon it was high above the ground, circling over the children's hut. A few minutes later it was gone, and the children knew that their brother was happy at last.

The Snag

Ted Hughes

Right from the beginning Eel was grey. And his wife was grey. And his children were grey.

They lived in the bed of the river under a stone. There they lay, loosely folded together, Eel and his wife, and two of his children. They breathed, and they waited, under a big stone.

Eel could peer out. He saw the water insects skittering about over the gravel, and sometimes swimming up through the water, to disappear through a ring of ripples. Where did they go?

He saw the bellies of the trout, the dace, the minnows, and one salmon, hovering in the current, or resting on the points of the stones on the river bed, their fins astir endlessly.

All day he lay under the dark stone.

But at night, when the sun went behind the wood, and the river grew suddenly dark, he slipped out. His wife and his two children followed him. Their noses were keener than any dog's. They could smell every insect. They rootled in the gravel of the river pool, nipping up the insects.

But wherever he went over the river bed, he heard the cry: "Here comes the grey snake! Look out for the grey snake! The grey snake is out! Watch for your babies!"

The fish could see him. Even in the dark, the fish with their luminous eyes could see him very well. They darted close, to see him better.

"Here he is!" piped a trout, in a thin treble

voice. "He's coming upstream. Horrible eyes is coming upstream."

And then: "Here he is!" chattered the minnows. "He's turning back downstream."

Wherever he moved, the fish kept up their cries: "Here's the grey snake now. Here he comes! Watch your babies!"

Eel pretended not to care. He poked his nose under the pebbles, picking out the insects. But the endless pestering got on his nerves. And his two children were frightened. "We're not snakes," he would shout. "We may be grey, but we're fish."

Then all the fish began to laugh, so the river pool shook. "Fish are silver," they cried. "Or green, or gold, or speckled, with pinky fins. Fish are beautiful. Fish have scales. They are shaped like fish. But you are grey. You have no scales. And you are a snake. Snake! Snake! Snake!"

They would begin to chant it all together, opening and closing their mouths. And Eel and his wife and children would finally glide back under their stone and lie hidden.

In a few minutes the fish would forget about them.

If there had been anywhere else to go, Eel would have gone there, to escape the fish of that pool. Once he did take his wife downstream, to a much bigger, deeper pool. But that was worse. Nearly thirty big salmon lay there, as well as many trout and dace and minnows. The salmon had shattering voices. They were used to calling to each other out on the stormy high seas. And now when Eel came slithering from under his stone, when night fell, a deafening chorus met him:

"Here comes the grey snake. Here he comes to eat your children. Here he comes. Watch out!"

And all the time he was hunting they kept it up: "Go home, grey snake! Go home, grey snake!"

Finally Eel led his family back to the smaller pool, where there was only one salmon.

His two children stopped going out at night. They lay curled up under the stone, crying. "What are we?" they sobbed. "Are we really grey snakes? If we aren't fish, what are we?"

Eel scowled and tried to comfort them. But he couldn't help worrying. "What if I am a grey snake, after all? How can I prove I'm a fish?"

Eel had only one friend, a lamprey. Lamprey was quite like Eel, but he was so ugly he didn't worry about anything. "I know I'm a horror," he would say. "But so what? Being ugly makes you smart."

One day this lamprey said to Eel: "I know a fortune-teller. She could tell you what you are. Why don't you ask her?"

Eel reared up like a swan. "A fortune-teller," he cried. "Why didn't you tell me?"

"I've told you," said Lamprey.

This fortune-teller, it turned out, was the new moon. "How can the new moon tell fortunes?" asked Eel.

"She tells fortunes only for a few minutes each day," explained Lamprey. "You have to get to her just as she touches the sea's edge, going down. Then she tells fortunes until she sinks out of sight. You have to listen very carefully. You don't hear her with your ears. You hear her with your thoughts."

"Let's go," said Eel. And he wanted to set off that minute downstream, but Lamprey checked him.

"Take a witness," said Lamprey.

"A witness?" asked Eel. "What for?"

"Unless you have a witness to what the new moon says, the fish will never believe you. Take the salmon."

The salmon was so sure the new moon would tell Eel he was really a snake, and not a fish at all, that he was eager to come. "I want to hear that," he cried. "I'll bring the truth back. Then you can stay out there in the sea, you needn't come back at all. It's the truth we want, not you."

So they set off. It was quite a journey, getting to the new moon. But finally Eel got there, with Lamprey beside him, to keep his spirits up, and, skulking behind, the salmon.

The new moon was actually a smile

without a face. It lay on the sea's rim like a face on a pillow. And the Smile smiled as Eel told his problem. It smiled as it sank slowly.

"You are a fish," said the Smile. "Not only are you a fish. You are a fish that God made for himself. God made you for himself."

"Me?" cried Eel. "God made me for himself? Why?"

"Because," said the Smile, "you are the sweetest of all the fish."

The salmon slammed the water with his tail. He'd always thought he was the sweetest. This was bad news on top of bad news.

"Say that again," cried the Eel.

"You are the sweetest of all the fish," said the Smile. It spoke so loud the whole sea chimed like a gong with the words.

Eel didn't know what to say. "Thank you," he stammered. "Oh, thank you." He was thinking how his children would jump up and down, as much as they could under their rock, when he told them this.

"But," said the Smile, as it sank. It seemed to be sinking faster and faster. There was only a little horn of light left, a little bright thorn, sticking above the sea.

"But?" cried the Eel. "But what?"

"There's a snag," said the Smile, and vanished.

"What snag? What's the snag?" cried Eel.

But the Smile had gone. The sea looked darker and colder. A shoal of flying fish burst upwards with a shivering laugh, and splashed back in again.

Still, Eel had what he wanted. And both Lamprey and Salmon were witnesses. Salmon had already gone, furious, as Eel and Lamprey set off home.

Back in the pool, Eel called all the fish together and told them exactly what had been said, "I am a fish," he said. "Not only that, I am God's favourite fish. God made me for himself. Because among all the fish, I am the sweetest."

"It is true," said the lamprey. "I was there."

"Yes," said the salmon. "Perhaps she did say that. But what did she mean? That's what I'd like to know. What did she mean?"

Even so, the fish were impressed. They didn't like it, but they were impressed. And from that moment, Eel and his wife and children surged about the pool throughout the day as well as the night. "Make way for God's own fish," he would shout, and butt the salmon. "Make way for the sweetest!"

The fish didn't know what to do. The story soon got about. The heron and the kingfisher told it to the birds. The otter told it to the animals. A crowd of them came to Man, and told him what had happened.

Man, who was drinking very sour cider, which he had just made out of crab-apples, pondered.

"What," he said finally, "does the eel mean by sweetest? How sweetest? Sweetest what? Sweetest nature?"

All the creatures became thoughtful. Then they became wildly excited.

"Man's got it!" they cried. "What does the horrible eel mean by sweetest? Sweetest how?"

The fish came crowding around Eel and his family. "Sweetest what?" they shouted.

"How are you sweetest? Come and prove you're the sweetest! You and your hideous infants. You and your goblin wife."

"It's a riddle," said the salmon. "The new moon posed a riddle. What does sweetest mean?"

"We are sweeter than any eel," cried the flowers. And the wild roses and the honeysuckles poured their perfumes over the river.

"And we are sweeter than any dumb eel," cried the thrushes, the blackbirds, the robins, the wrens, and they poured out their brilliant songs over the river.

"And my children are the sweetest of all the animals," cried the otter, holding up its kittens.

"They are not," cried the sheep, and she butted forward her two lambs.

"No, they are not," cried the fox, suddenly standing there with a woolly cub.

"Among the fish," cried the eel. "That's what she said. I am the sweetest among the fish. Who cares about perfumes? Who wants to smell? And who cares about song? What counts is the thought. And who cares about fluffy darlings? The otter grows up to murder eels. The lamb grows up to butcher the flowers. The fox-cub grows up to murder the mice. What sort of sweetness is that? No. My sweetness is the real sweetness, the sort that God loves best."

"Taste?" asked Man. "That leaves only taste."

Eel would have blinked, if he had had eyelids. Taste? He hadn't thought of that.

"That's it!" shouted the fish, sticking their heads out of the water. "Taste! Cook us and eat us, see who's the sweetest. Taste us all. Taste us all!"

Eel felt suddenly afraid. Who was going to taste him? Was Man going to cook him? But the fish were shouting to Man: "You can eat one of each of us. And then eat Eel as well, and then you can judge. Here we are. Here we are."

The fish were quite ready to let one of each kind of them be eaten so long as it meant that Eel too would be eaten.

"No," cried Eel. "Wait."

But fish were jumping ashore. One trout, one dace, one minnow, and even that salmon – he too was offering himself. All to get the eel killed and eaten!

Eel twisted round and fled. But the otter plunged in after him. And in the swirling chase, the otter grabbed Eel's wife. She was much bigger than Eel anyway.

Eel coiled under the stone with his two children. He couldn't believe it. The oven was glowing, the fish were frying. And his wife too! It was terrible! But all he could do was stare and feel helpless.

And Man and Woman were already testing, with dainty forks and thin slices of buttered brown bread.

They didn't like Dace at all. He tasted of mud. The minnow was quite nice – but peculiar. The trout was fairly good – but a little too watery. He needed lemon and – and – something. And the salmon – the salmon, now! Well, the salmon seemed just about the most wonderful thing possible – till they tasted Eel.

Woman uttered a cry and almost dropped her fork. Tears came into her eyes and she stared at Man.

"Was there ever anything so delicious!" she gasped. "So sweet! So sweet!"

Man rested his brow on his hand.

"How have we lived so long," he said, "and not realized what gorgeous goodies lay down there, under the river-stones? How could anything be sweeter than this eel?"

"Eel!" he shouted. "You have won. God is right again. You are the sweetest!"

Eel heard and trembled. And he shrank back under the stone, deeper into the dark, when he heard Man say: "Bring me another!"

Otter came swirling down through the current. Otter was working for Man. Eel and his two children shot downstream. But one had to be hindmost. One of the children. And when Eel looked round, only one of his children was following.

And as they slipped and squirmed down through the shallows, among the stones, towards the next pool below, the heron

peered down out of heaven and – szwack!
The other eel-child was twisting in the
heron's long bill. The heron too was working
for Man.

But the eels were so sweet, neither Otter
nor Heron could resist eating them on the
spot. From that moment, the Otter hid from
Man and spent all his time hunting more
eels – for himself. And from that moment
Heron was afraid of Man – flapping up and
reeling away with a panicky "Aaaark" – only
to land somewhere else where he could go
on hunting eels – for himself. Neither Otter
nor Heron wanted to hand over what they
caught – eels were much too sweet!

But Eel himself hid from all of them. He
oiled his body, to make it hard to grip. And
whenever he sees the slightest glow of light
he hides deeper under the stones, or deeper
into the mud. He thinks it is Man searching
for him. Or he thinks it is the point of the
moon sinking and he suddenly remembers
THE SNAG.

Yes, the snag.

Hey, Danny!

Robin Klein

"Right," said Danny's mother sternly. "That school bag cost ten pounds. You can just save up your pocket money to buy another one. How could you possibly lose a big school bag, anyhow?"

"Dunno," said Danny. "I just bunged in some empty bottles to take back to the milkbar, and I was sort of swinging it round by the handles coming home, and it sort of fell over that culvert thing down on to a lorry on the motorway."

"And you forgot to write your name and phone number in it as I told you to," said Mrs Hillerey. "Well, you'll just have to use my blue weekend bag till you save up enough pocket money to replace the old one. And no arguments!"

Danny went and got the blue bag from the hall cupboard and looked at it.

The bag was not just blue; it was a vivid, clear, electric blue, like a flash of lightning. The regulation colour for schoolbags at his school was a khaki-olive- brown, inside and out, which didn't show stains from when your can of Coke leaked, or when you left your salami sandwiches uneaten and forgot about them for a month.

"I can't take this bag to school," said Danny. "Not one this colour. Can't I take my books and stuff in one of those green plastic rubbish bags?"

"Certainly not!" said Mrs Hillerey.

On Monday at the bus stop, the kids all stared at the blue bag.

"Hey," said Jim, who was supposed to be his mate. "That looks like one of those bags girls take to ballet classes."

"Hey, Danny, you got one of those frilly dresses in there?" asked Spike.

"Aw, belt up, can't you?" said Danny miserably. On the bus the stirring increased as more and more kids got on. It was a very long trip for Danny. It actually took only twenty minutes – when you had an ordinary brown schoolbag and not a great hunk of sky to carry round with you. Every time anyone spoke to him they called him "Little Boy Blue".

"It matches his lovely blue eyes," said one kid.

"Maybe he's got a little blue trike with training wheels too," said another kid.

"Hey, Danny, why didn't you wear some nice blue ribbons in your hair?"

When Danny got off the bus he made a dash for his classroom and shoved the bag under his desk. First period they had Miss Reynolds, and when she was marking the register she looked along the aisle and saw Danny's bag and said, "That's a very elegant bag you have there, Danny."

Everyone else looked round and saw the blue bag and began carrying on. Danny kept a dignified silence, and after five minutes Miss Reynolds made them stop singing "A life on the Ocean Waves". But all through maths and English, heads kept turning round to grin at Danny and his radiantly blue bag.

At break he sneaked into the art room and mixed poster paints into a shade of khaki-olive-brown which he rubbed over his bag with his hankie. When the bell rang he had a grey handkerchief, but the bag was still a clear and innocent blue. "Darn thing," Danny muttered in disgust. "Must be made of some kind of special waterproof atomic material. Nothing sticks to it."

"What are you doing in the art room, Daniel?" asked Miss Reynolds. "And what is that terrible painty mess?"

"I was just painting a Zodiac sign on my bag," said Danny.

"I wish you boys wouldn't write things all over your good school bags. Clean up that mess, Danny, and go to your next lesson."

But Danny said he was feeling sick and could he please lie down in the sick bay for a while. He sneaked his blue bag in with him, and found the key to the first-aid box and looked inside for something that would turn bright blue bags brown. There was a little bottle of brown lotion, so Danny tipped the whole lot on to cotton wool and scrubbed it into the surface of the bag. But the lotion just ran off the bag and went all over his hands and the bench top in the sick bay.

"Danny Hillerey!" said the school secretary. "You know very well that no pupil is allowed to unlock the first-aid box. What on earth are you doing?"

"Sorry," said Danny. "Just looking for some liver salts."

"I think you'd better sit quietly out in the fresh air if you feel sick," Mrs Adams said suspiciously. "And who owns that peculiar-looking blue bag?"

"It belongs in the sports equipment shed," said Danny. "It's got measuring tapes and stuff in it. Blue's our house colour."

He went and sat outside with the bag shoved under the seat and looked at it and despaired. Kids from his class started going down to the oval for games, and they started in on him again.

Danny glared and said "Get lost" and "Drop dead". Then Miss Reynolds came along and made him go down to the oval with the others.

On the way there Danny sloshed the blue bag in a puddle of mud – but nothing happened, the blue became shinier, if anything. He also tried grass stains under the sprinkler, which had the same effect. Amongst the line-up of khaki-olive-brown bags, his blue one was as conspicuous as a Clydesdale horse in a herd of small ponies.

"Hey, Danny, what time's your tap dancing lesson?" said the kids.

"Hey, Danny, where did you get that knitting bag? I want to buy one for my aunty."

"Hey, Danny, when did you join the Bluebell marching girls' squad?"

141

Finally Danny had had enough.

"This bag's very valuable, if you want to know," he said.

"Rubbish," everyone scoffed. "It's just an ordinary old vinyl bag."

"I had to beg my mum to let me bring that bag to school," said Danny. "It took some doing, I can tell you. Usually she won't let it out of the house."

"Why?" demanded everyone. "What's so special about it?"

Danny grabbed his bag and wiped off the traces of mud and poster paint and brown lotion and grass stains. The bag was stained inside where all that had seeped in through the seams and the zip, and it would take some explaining when his mother noticed it. (Which she would, next time she went to spend the weekend at Grandma's.) There was her name inside, E. Hillerey, in big neat letters. E for Enid.

"Well," said Danny, "that bag belonged to . . . well, if you really want to know, it went along on that expedition up Mount Everest."

Everyone jeered.

"It did so," said Danny. "Look, Sir Edmund Hillary, there's his name printed right there inside. And there's a reason it's this funny colour. So it wouldn't get lost in the snow. It was the bag Sir Edmund Hillary carried that flag in they stuck up on top of Mount Everest. But I'm not going to bring it to school any more if all you can do is poke fun at the colour."

Everyone went all quiet and respectful.

"Wow," said Jeff in an awed voice, and he touched the letters that Danny's mother had written with a laundry marking pencil.

"Gosh," said Mark. "We never knew you were related to that Sir Edmund Hillary."

Danny looked modest. "We're only distantly related," he admitted. "He's my dad's second cousin."

"Hey, Danny, can I hold it on the bus? I'll be really careful with it."

"Hey, Danny, can I have a turn when you bring it to school tomorrow?"

"I'll charge you ten pence a go," said Danny.

"That's fair, for a bag that went up to the top of Mount Everest."

"Ten pence a kid," he calculated. "One hundred kids at ten pence a turn, ten pounds. A new brown school bag. And with a bit of luck, I'll earn all that before someone checks up in the library and finds out Sir Edmund Hillary's name's spelt differently!"

The Bakerloo Flea

Michael Rosen

Not long ago I was in a pub round the Elephant and Castle, and I got talking to a woman, an oldish woman. And we were talking about this and that, and she said she used to be a cleaner down the Underground. I didn't know, but it seems as if every night after the last tube, they switch the electric current off and teams of night-cleaners go through the Underground, along the tunnels, cleaning up all the muck, rubbish, fag ends and stuff that we chuck on to the lines. They sweep out between the lines on one station, and then, in a gang of about six or seven, walk on to the next station along the lines in the tunnels.

Anyway this woman (I don't know her name), she says to me:

"Did you ever hear talk of the Bakerloo flea?"

"Bakerloo flea?" I said. "No, no, never."

"Well," she said, "you know there are rats down there – down the Underground? Hundreds of 'em. And the thing is," she said, "is that some of them have grown enormous. Huge great big things."

"I've heard of them," I said. "Super rats."

"Right," she says. "Now you tell me," she says, "what lives on rats? Fleas, right? Fleas. So – the bigger the rats the bigger the fleas. Stands to reason. These rats, they feed on all the old garbage that people throw down on the lines. It's amazing what people throw away, you know."

She told me they found a steak down there once, lipstick, a bowler hat, beads, a box of eggs and hundreds and hundreds of sweets – especially Maltesers and those balls of bubble gum you get out of slot machines.

Anyway, the rats eat these, get big, and it seems that one day they were working the Bakerloo Line – Elephant and Castle to Paddington – and just before Baker Street one of the women in the gang was looking ahead, and she screamed out:

"Look – look – what's that?" Up in front was a great, grey, spiky thing with huge hairy legs and big jaws. It was as big as a big dog – bigger.

And the moment she screamed, it jumped away from them, making a sort of grating, scraping noise. Well, they were scared stiff. Scared stiff. But they had to finish the job, so they carried on up the line to Paddington. But they didn't see it again that night or the next, or the next.

Some of them thought they'd imagined it, because it can get very spooky down there. They sing and shout a lot she told me, and tell saucy jokes, not fit for my ears.

Anyway, about a fortnight later, at the

same place – just before Baker Street on the Bakerloo Line – suddenly one of them looks up and there it was again. A great, big, grey, spiky thing with long legs and big jaws.

"It's a flea, sure to God it's a flea," one of them said.

The moment it heard this, again it jumped. Again, they heard this scraping, grating sound, and it disappeared down the tunnel – in the dark. They walked on, Baker Street, Marylebone, Edgware Road, to Paddington. Nothing.

Anyway – this time they had a meeting. They decided it *was* a flea, a gigantic flea, and it must have grown up from a family of fleas that had lived for years and years growing bigger and bigger, sucking the blood of all the fat rats down there.

So they decided that it was time to tell one of the high-ups in London Transport, or they wouldn't go down there any more.

For a start-off, no one'd believe them.

"Just a gang of women seeing things in the dark," the supervisor said.

Right! One of them had a bright idea. She said:

"I'll tell you what we'll do – we'll tell them that we're coming out on strike, and we'll tell the papers about the flea, the Bakerloo flea. It'll be a huge scandal – no one'll dare go by tube, it'll be a national scandal."

So they threatened the manager with this, and this time the high-ups really moved. They were so scared the story might get out, and they'd be blamed, and one of them would lose his job.

So for a start they stopped all cleaning on the Bakerloo line, and one of the high-ups went down the tunnel with the women. You can just see it, can't you? Four in the morning, a gang of six women with feather dusters, and one of the bowler hat and briefcase brigade walking down the tunnel on the hunt for the Bakerloo flea. Sounded incredible to me.

Anyway, it seems as if they came round that same corner just before Baker Street and the woman had gone quiet and the bloke was saying: "If this is a hoax, if this is a trick . . ." when they heard that awful, hollow, scraping noise.

At first they couldn't see it, but then – there it was – not *between* the lines this time – *on* the lines – a gigantic flea. No question, that's what it was.

Well, he took one look at it, and next moment he was backing off.

"Back, ladies, back. Back, ladies!"

Of course *he* was more scared than they were. Terrified. But he was even more terrified when one of the women let out this scream. Not because *she* was scared, but to scare off the flea. And it worked. It jumped. Right out of sight.

Well, there was no carrying on up the line that night.

"Back, ladies, back," was all he could say, and back they went.

Next thing they knew, they were all called into an office with a carpet and the Queen on the wall. And there was a whole gang of these men.

First thing, one of them says, they weren't to let anyone know of this, no one at all must ever hear of what they had all seen. There was no point in letting a panic develop. Anyway, next he says:

"We haven't let the grass grow under our feet. We've got a scientist with us."

And then the scientist, he says:

"I've got this powder. Deadly flea powder. All you need to do is spread this up and down the Bakerloo Line, and there'll be no more trouble with this flea thing."

Well, the woman in the pub – I never found out her name – said:

"So who's going to spread this stuff about down there? The army?"

"No," the man said. "We don't see any need for that. You," he says, "you."

"So there's a fine one," the woman said to me. "First of all they said it was just a bunch of women afraid of the dark, then they send Tarzan in pinstripes down there and he can't get out fast enough, and now it's us that has to spread this flea powder.

"Well," she said, "we knew it wouldn't be any good anyway. Flea powder never is."

They took it down there, threw it about between Regent's Park and Baker Street and Edgware Road – while up above, in the big houses, ambassadors from all over the world slept soundly in their beds. They told them not to go down for a week, and not to breathe a word of it to anyone.

"They were more scared of a story in the papers than we were of the flea," she said.

It hadn't attacked anyone, no one had seen it there in daytime, so down they went. But there it was again – sitting there just before Baker Street, with some of the powder sticking to the hairs on its legs. But this time, instead of hopping away down the line, it turned and faced them. They turned and ran, and then it leapt. It leapt at the women, and they ran back down the tunnel to Regent's Park. This great, grey flea was trying to get at them.

"We screamed," she said, "we really screamed, but it was after us, 'cos you see that damned flea powder hadn't killed the flea – it had killed the rats. It was starving for fresh blood. Probably *mad* for blood, by

now," she said. "We ran and ran and the flea was hopping – but it was hitting the roof of the tunnel, it was so mad to get at us. There was this terrible scraping sound of its shell on the roof of the tunnel, and it'd fall back on to the lines. So we could move faster than it. We rushed back to Regent's Park, and calls went up and down the line and all over the system to lock the gates on every station and seal the system. Seal off the Underground system of London. Well, it was about four o'clock – two hours to go before a million people would be down there.

"What were they going to do? Upstairs in the office they were in a blind panic. They could've done something about it earlier, instead of fobbing us off. They couldn't call in the army without telling the Minister, and if they told the Minister, he'd tell the Prime Minister, and all the high-ups would get the sack. So they had this plan to turn the current on, and run the maintenance train at high speed through the tunnel from Paddington to the Elephant and Castle, in the hope that it would get killed beneath the wheels of the train, or smashed against the buffers at the Elephant.

"They did it. They sent it through. Of course *that* didn't work. We knew it wouldn't work. Anyone that's lived with a flea knows you can't squash fleas – you've got to crack 'em. They're hard, rock hard.

"After the maintenance man ran the maintenance train through, they went down to the gates at Regent's Park, and they stood and listened, and from down below they could hear the grating, scraping noise of its shell on its legs. Of course, it was obvious now why it had stuck to this stretch of the line all the time. Some of the juiciest rubbish was in the bins round those posh parts, so you got the biggest rats, so that was where you got the great Bakerloo flea.

"So now they had less than two hours to get rid of the flea, or leave it for a day and run the risk of letting a million people down into the tunnels to face a flea, starving, starving for blood, or shutting the whole system down and telling everyone to go by bus.

"Well, you know what happened?" she said. "*We* did it. *We* got rid of it."

"You did?"

"Yes, we did it. Vera's old man worked on the dustcarts for Camden council. She knew how to kill the flea. It was Vera's plan that what we'd do was go down, actually down on to the line at Oxford Circus with dustbin lids, banging them with brushes and broom handles, and drive the flea back up the line to Queen's Park where the Bakerloo Line comes out of the tunnel into the open air. And at Queen's Park, Vera's old man and his gang would have a couple of carts backed up into the tunnel. And that's what we did. We got driven to Vera's place to get her old man up, on to his mates' places to get them up, then they went to the council builders' yard to get boards, builders' planks. We got the lids off the bins, and down we went. Oxford Circus, Regent's Park, Baker Street, Marylebone, Edgware Road, Paddington and we shouted and we banged, and we banged and we shouted every step of the way.

"We saw it just once at Edgware Road waiting for us, but we walked together, holding the lids up in front of us like shields, and it was as if it knew it couldn't get at us this time, 'cos it turned – it had just room to turn in the tunnel – and as we came up to Queen's Park still banging and shouting, it leapt – not at us, but at one of the carts. Alongside it was the other one, between the wheels were the boards, some of them stacked up to block off all the gaps. The flea was trapped between us with our lids and the back of the dustcarts. It leapt, it hit the roof of the tunnel, just like it did when it chased us. We shouted and banged. It leapt again. This time we had it. It was in the back of the dustcart.

"We kept up the banging and the shouting. We got as near to the back of the dustcart as we could. We could see it there, every hair of its legs, and Vera shouts:

"Turn it on, Bob, turn it on," and Bob turned on the masher (they call it 'The Shark'), in the back of his cart. And it bit into the back of that flea like giant nails crunching through eggshells. The smell was revolting. Bit by bit, the flea was dragged into the cart. We could see it as it went: first its body, then its legs. I'll never forget the sight of those huge hairy legs twitching about in the back of Bob's cart, Vera shouting:

"'You've got him, love, you've got him!'

"He had, too. That was that. That was the end of the Bakerloo flea. But do you know, when we got up to the top, that load from head office were there. They were crying, crying out of relief, crying their eyes out. Twenty minutes later, hundreds and thousands of people were down there, off to work, none the wiser. They didn't know about any flea, any Bakerloo flea. They don't even know we go down there every night cleaning up their mess for them. Of course, head office made us promise never to breathe a word of it. We promised.

"Vera said: 'What's it worth to you?'

"He said: 'Your honour. Your word. And your word's your honour.'

"And they gave us a week's extra holiday

tagged on to August Bank Holiday that year."

She told me I was the first person she'd ever told the story to, and told me never to tell anyone. The scandal would be terrible. I don't know whether to believe her or not.

Marrow Hill

Jan Mark

All the Burton children looked barmy. They had mad gleeful faces and wild weak eyes behind thick glasses, through which they ogled like loony goldfish. They all wore glasses. There seemed to be ten of them, twenty swivelling eyes, but it was possible to count them when they stopped moving and there were only four after all; eight eyes.

I saw the Burtons once a year, when I went to stay with my Aunt Eileen for two weeks, in the summer holidays. Aunt Eileen lived in a street that was just like our street, in a town that was just like ours. The only thing that turned the visit into a holiday was the hour-long journey there by bus. Once I got off the bus, everything was much the same as it was at home, except for the Burtons.

The Burtons lived next door to Aunt Eileen. All the other back gardens in the street had palings round them, no more than waist height, but the Burtons were surrounded by a tall corrugated iron fence with woundy-looking spikes on top.

"To stop them getting out," said Aunt Eileen, who lived next door to them all the year round. In the front garden the Burtons' privet hedge grew high and secretive, screening the bay window where the blinds were always down. After I had been staying with Aunt Eileen for three consecutive summers, I knew all the neighbours in her row, but none of them knew the Burtons. They were like a rare and unpredictable species in a cage at the zoo; you looked, but you didn't poke your fingers through the bars.

I did my looking from an upstairs window. If I went into the bathroom and stood on the Lloyd Loom laundry-basket, I could see over the corrugated iron fence into the Burtons' garden, and almost into their back room, through the french windows. Even when the windows were open the curtains were drawn, but sometimes, when a Burton came out, I got a glimpse of a bamboo table and a hairy rug like a dead dog that had been shot down on the threshold while defending its master.

By leaning far out I could see right down to the end of the Burtons' garden. They had an ash tree in the corner and the grass grew long like meadow grass. I suppose that it had been a lawn once, because there was a dent in the middle that might have been a flowerbed. The iron fence was overgrown with blackberry vines that straggled across to our side in places, although the berries were never black when I was there.

One summer the Burtons had a tent. We had a tent at home which my father put up for us when we could persuade him, but the

Burtons erected their own. They tried to. Eldest Burton stood in the middle and gave orders while the other three, or nine, milled round him with guy-lines and tent-pegs and a mallet with which they crushed their own and each others' fingers.

The two middle Burtons were girls. They jumped up and down a lot, shrieking: "Oh, I say! What shall I do with this? Oh, I say! What have you done with that? Oh, get out of the way, you ass. You drip. You clot. You wet. You utter weed! Oh! Oh! Oh!"

"Oh, shut up!" yelled Eldest Burton, laying about him with the ridge-pole.

"Oh, don't be beastly, Specs," the others screamed, and threw themselves down to roll in the long grass, waving their legs in the air and braying.

I thought they had a nerve, calling him Specs, because as I said, they all wore glasses. If he had a proper name, they never used it, and he never used theirs. They called each other Specs, Tiddy, Bunny, Twizzle and Smudge, quite arbitrarily. He who was Smudge one day might be Twizzle the next. I could never tell which was which, and when they lost their tempers they were all drips, clots, asses, wets and utter weeds.

Even their mother didn't seem to know their names. When she wanted them she stood at the top of the steps by the back door and called them collectively: "Darleengs!" and they would drop whatever they were doing, usually each other, and swarm up the garden like lemmings, breathless and still yelling.

"What, Mummy, what, Mummy; Mummy, Mummy, what?"

Some days they played cricket. They always began very seriously, setting up stumps and excavating a crease in the jungle vegetation. The bowler had to begin his run inside the back room, burst through the french windows, down the steps and let go the ball at the top of the rockery, which was overgrown to the point where it looked like the foothills of the Himalayas. This delivery was followed by a reverberant clang as the ball hit the iron fence, for the Burtons' cricket season was one long succession of maiden overs – except once. Once, Youngest Burton kept his bat down and hit a six. I saw the ball descend among Aunt Eileen's tomato plants.

I leaped off the linen basket, ran downstairs and out into the garden. I couldn't believe my luck – at last, a chance to meet them. We might talk. I reached the garden path. I stopped.

There was a Burton in Aunt Eileen's tomatoes.

It was Elder Middle Burton. Younger Middle Burton and Youngest Burton were astride the iron fence, in horrid danger of being impaled on the spikes.

"Do you want your ball?" I said, coldly.

Elder Middle Burton sprang out of the tomatoes, whooping like a klaxon with laughter, or simple insanity, and went up the fence the way a cat goes up curtains. All three Burtons vanished simultaneously and I heard them recounting their adventures to Eldest.

"Oh! Oh! I say! Specs . . . in the garden

... oh! There's – a – funny – little – girl!"

That was me.

"I'm not half as funny as you are!" I yelled, and went indoors, hating them. But I was soon back on the laundry-basket.

Aunt Eileen let me sleep in her big front bedroom, in the big swampy double bed that she had once shared with my uncle. His name had been Percy, but he had died before I knew him, and I always thought of him as Uncle Eileen. From the window in that room I could watch Father and Mother Burton set off on evening excursions.

Father would come out first, jangling keys as though he were about to leap into a powerful car and roar away. I don't think they had a car at all; he went to work on a sit-up-and-beg push-bike. Then Mother Burton floated down the path, all draped in white like a night-scented flower that attracts moths. She would stand at the gate, keening farewells to the mob who hung out of the windows – surely there were ten of them at night – rattling the wooden slats of the venetian blinds like castanets, while her thin high voice spiralled eerily above the yoiks and tally-hoes of her offspring.

"Goodbye, my darleengs. Take care of each other for Mummy. Goodbyeee!"

"You would think," said Aunt Eileen, peering over my shoulder, "that they were going to the opera."

Mother and Father Burton moved off; he subfusc and already lost in the shadows, she catching the last of the sunset and glimmering up the road.

"Where are they going, then?" I said, as the Burtons slammed down every single front window, one after the other. These thuds were followed by a dislocated clatter as the venetian blinds descended.

"To the Odeon, probably," said Aunt Eileen. "There's a good film on, this week. Shall we go, tomorrow?"

I lay in bed, looking forward to that, and listening to the thumps and crashes next door, which was the Burtons taking care of each other for Mummy.

A few days later they got hold of a camera. It was a square black box with bits sticking out of the sides, and it looked like a device for detonating gelignite. The camera seemed to be common property, like their clothes which appeared indiscriminately on each Burton in turn, and they fought savagely over it, while carrying on the usual conversation.

"Oh! Filthy pig! *My turn*. Bags I next. Rotten beast!" Knuckles rang against teeth. "Utter weed! *My* turn. Oh! Ouch! Leggo!"

"Yarroo," murmured Aunt Eileen, passing by with clean towels.

Sometime towards the middle of the afternoon, one of the Burtons actually got its hands on the camera for long enough to make the others line up and be photographed. They draped their arms round each other and smiled with lolling heads, so that they looked as if they had all been garrotted. For once I felt as though

I shouldn't be looking, as though I had witnessed something that ordinary people shouldn't see.

It was the strangest sight. They seemed to be pretending to be children so that they could display the photograph and say, "Look. This proves it. We're real." But they didn't look real, and the longer they stood there, the less real they looked; not only pretending to be children, but pretending to be alive. After the shutter had clicked there was another fight and the camera was flung into the rockery where it fell against a stone and burst open. At that moment, Mother Burton began her banshee routine at the top of the steps and they all thundered indoors. I fetched Uncle Eileen's army fieldglasses and took a closer look at the camera. There was no film in it.

I was almost convinced then that the Burtons were ghosts, and not children's ghosts: grown-up ghosts doing all the things that they thought children should do. But next day Youngest Burton cut his chin on the door-scraper while biting his sister on the leg, and bled real blood, so that theory was no good. All the same, I began to watch to see if they had shadows. It was hard to tell, they moved so fast. I decided that they had only one shadow between them, like the weird sisters with their single eye.

That was the year they got the tortoise.

I knew from the start that they had made a grave mistake with that tortoise. It was the wrong pet. When it arrived they put it down in the grass and danced round it, singing a tortoise-warming song. They called it Flash, which was supposed to be a joke, I think. They treated it as one of themselves, pushing it about like a toy tank and howling encouragement but, wisely, it wouldn't come out. I imagine that they hoped to train it to jump through hoops and fetch sticks, and I wondered what would happen when they discovered that it wouldn't cooperate; but before it could be persuaded to join them at cricket, it got under the iron fence and went to live three doors down with the Rodgerses, who knew when to keep their mouths shut.

They tried again the following year, and this time they got it right. They got a dog and it was the right kind of dog, curly-tailed and hysterical. It was a proper children's-book dog; they called it Sammy, which was the right kind of name, and it behaved in the right kind of way, woofing and barking, leaping off the ground on all four legs at once and looking up at the Burtons with intelligent doggy eyes when they told it secrets.

"Oh! *Angel* – Sammy. He understands *everything* we say," they bawled at each other. Most of the time, though, they bawled at the dog.

"Fetch Sammy! Catch, Sammy! Beg, Sammy! Die for the King, Sammy!" The King was already dead, but Sammy lay down anyway, dead as the hairy rug by the french windows. I wondered if they had text books: *How to be a Child: How to be a Child with a Dog*. Sammy clearly had one too: *How to be a Children's Dog*.

There was so much riot in the Burtons' garden that it was several days before I noticed that one Burton was missing, and a little longer before I realized that it was always the same one. From time to time Eldest Burton would disappear. I never saw him go or come back, and for a while I supposed that he was dematerializing behind the ash tree.

The Burtons had a back gate, but they didn't go through it, any more than they went through the front gate. They were contained. Aunt Eileen had a back gate too, opening on to the mud path along the ends of the gardens, and on the other side of the path were allotments. One day I went through our gate just as Eldest Burton was climbing over his. I drew back into the garden until he was well clear, and then followed at a canny distance. A Burton on the loose: was society at risk?

Eldest Burton went under a bulge in the chain-link fence and made off into the plantation of pea-sticks and bean rows, through a froth of cauliflowers and behind the raspberry-canes. Now, there was a wasted opportunity. It occurred to me that if the Burtons hoped to pass for real children, they ought to be out raiding the allotments every day, but possibly they had not yet reached the chapter on scrumping in the text book. Eldest Burton kept going until he got to the place where the ground fell away towards the flour mill and the river. There was an old Nissen hut here, and I crept round it, keeping my head well down behind the nettles and fat hen plants. I rather hoped to catch him changing back into whatever he was really – not a child – but when I reached the end of the Nissen hut, he was just sitting still with his back to me. He was sitting on a mound of earth surrounded by vegetable marrows.

I trod on an old cloche that broke up with a crunch, and he looked round.

"What do you want?" he said. That was all he said, and he just said it, in an ordinary voice, like people did who weren't Burtons. I was so surprised, I couldn't think of a lie.

"I was following you," I said.

"You live next door, don't you?" he said.

"Sometimes I stay with my Aunt Eileen in the summer holidays."

This was the cue for him to bounce up on end and shriek, "Hooray for the Hols!" which was exactly what he would have done in his own back garden, but he didn't.

"I thought I didn't see you very often," he said.

I thought that was putting it mildly. Where did he imagine I got to during the other fifty weeks of the year?

"Are you going to make a row?" he said.

"No."

"Then welcome to Marrow Hill. Come on up."

I went on up, between the marrow plants, and sat down beside him at the top. There was a kind of flat hard place to sit on. I guessed that he must have worn it smooth and that he came here often.

"Are these your marrows?"

"No."

"Your dad's, I mean."

"He doesn't grow things."

I thought of the garden behind the iron fence. "No."

"He grew a nasturtium, once."

"What happened to it?"

"He killed it," said Eldest Burton, and I imagined Father Burton with a shotgun, waiting behind the hedge for the nasturtium to come round the corner. "It took so long to come up, he forgot what it was. He thought it was a weed."

"Well, whose marrows are they?"

"I don't know," he said. "It doesn't matter. I don't do them any harm. They know me." I wasn't sure that I had heard him aright. "Look at this one." He patted the largest marrow of all. "This is old man Grimshaw."

"*Who?*"

"Old Grimshaw; he's the gaffer. I knew him when he was that long." Eldest Burton indicated something the size of a chipolata sausage between thumb and forefinger. "And this is Adelaide Bulk. That's Henry the Eighth and here – " he moved some leaves and uncovered a welter-weight and a runt, " – are Laurel and Hardy. Look behind you."

I looked. There crouched a marrow so variously striped that it seemed to be stuffed into a tartan skin.

"Wee Hamish McBagpipe."

He introduced me to every marrow on the mound, right down to the Babe-in-Arms who was one inch long and still had a flower on the end. It turned out that the marrows were all related; all descended from Gaffer Grimshaw, and Eldest Burton kindly explained who was whose father, aunt, cousin, nephew. I noticed that there didn't seem to be any brothers or sisters among them. Then he sat back, resting on his elbows, and whistled quietly. He whistled "Christians, Awake", which was an odd choice for August as it usually gets sung on Christmas morning. I half expected the marrows to be charmed and rise up on gently swaying stalks.

Perhaps he *was* barmy; not Burton-barmy but plain honest-to-goodness round the bend. Perhaps I should humour him.

"Don't you find them a bit boring?" I asked, looking at his supine friends.

"No." He seemed surprised. "Of course they're not boring."

"But you can't – well, you can't play cricket with marrows, can you?"

"No," he agreed happily. "You can't."

"And they don't talk to you, do they?"

"No."

"What do they do, then?" I asked.

"Do?" said Eldest Burton. He smiled blissfully. "They don't do anything."

Such a Sweet Little Girl

Lance Salway

It was at breakfast on a bright Saturday morning that Julie first made her announcement. She put down her spoon, swallowed a last mouthful of cornflakes, and said, "There's a ghost in my bedroom."

No one took any notice. Her mother was writing a shopping list and her father was deep in his newspaper. Neither of them heard what she said. Her brother Edward heard but he ignored her, which is what he usually did. Edward liked to pretend that

Julie didn't exist. It wasn't easy but he did his best.

Julie tried again. She raised her voice and said, "There's a ghost in my bedroom."

Mrs Bennett looked up from her list. "Is there, dear? Oh, good. Do you think we need more marmalade? And I suppose I'd better buy a cake or something if your friends are coming to tea."

Edward said sharply, "Friends? What friends?"

"Sally and Rachel are coming to tea with Julie this afternoon," his mother said.

Edward gave a loud theatrical groan. "Oh, no. Why does she have to fill the house with her rotten friends?"

"You could fill the house with *your* friends, too," Julie said sweetly. "If you had any."

Edward looked at her with loathing. "Oh, I've got friends all right," he said. "I just don't inflict them on other people."

"You haven't got any friends," Julie said quietly. "You haven't got any friends because no one likes you."

"That's enough," Mr Bennett said, looking up from his paper, and there was silence then, broken only by the gentle rumble-slush, rumble-slush of the washing machine in the corner.

Edward chewed a piece of toast and thought how much he hated Julie. He hated a lot of people. Most people, in fact. But there were some he hated more than others. Mr Jenkins, who taught maths. And that woman in the paper shop who'd accused him of stealing chewing gum, when everyone knew he never touched the stuff. And Julie. He hated Julie most of all. He hated her pretty pale face and her pretty fair curls and her pretty little lisping voice. He hated the grown-ups who constantly fluttered round her, saying how enchanting she was, and so clever for her age, and wasn't Mrs Bennett lucky to have such a sweet little girl. What they didn't say, but he knew they were thinking it behind their wide bright smiles, was poor Mrs Bennett, with that lumpy, sullen boy. So different from his sister. So different from lovely little Julie.

Lovely little Julie flung her spoon on the table. "I *said* there's a ghost in my bedroom."

Mrs Bennett put down her shopping list and biro in order to give Julie her full attention. "Oh dear," she said. "I hope it didn't frighten you, darling."

Julie smiled and preened. "No," she said smugly. "*I* wasn't frightened."

Edward tried to shut his ears. He knew this dialogue by heart. The Bennett family spent a great deal of time adjusting their habits to suit Julie's fantasies. Once, for a whole month, they had all been forced to jump the bottom tread of the staircase because Julie insisted that two invisible rabbits were sleeping there. For a time she had been convinced, or so she said, that a pink dragon lived in the airing cupboard. And there had been a terrible few weeks the year before when all communication with her had to be conducted through an invisible fairy called Priscilla who lived on her left shoulder.

And now there was a ghost in her bedroom.

Try as he might, Edward couldn't shut out his sister's voice. On and on it whined: ". . . I was really very brave and didn't run away even though it was so frightening, and I said . . ."

Edward looked at his parents with contempt. His father had put down the newspaper and was gazing at Julie with a soppy smile on his face. His mother was wearing the mock-serious expression that adults often adopt in order to humour their young. Edward hated them for it. If he'd told them a story about a ghost when *he* was seven, they'd have told him to stop being so silly, there's no such thing as ghosts, why don't you grow up, be a man.

"What sort of ghost is it?" he asked suddenly.

Julie looked at him in surprise. Then her eyes narrowed. "It's a frightening ghost," she said. "With great big eyes and teeth and horrible, nasty claws. Big claws. And it smells."

"Ghosts aren't like that," Edward said scornfully. "Ghosts have clanking chains and skeletons, and they carry their heads under their arms."

"This ghost doesn't," Julie snapped.

"Funny sort of ghost, then."

"You don't know anything about it."

Julie's voice was beginning to tremble. Edward sighed. There'd be tears soon and he'd get the blame. As usual.

"Come now, Edward," his father said heartily. "It's only pretend. Isn't it, lovey?"

Lovey shot him a vicious glance. "It's *not* pretend. It's a real ghost. And it's in my bedroom."

"Of course, darling." Mrs Bennet picked up her shopping list again. "How are we off for chutney, I wonder?"

But Edward wasn't going to let the matter drop. Not this time. "Anyway," he said, "ghosts don't have claws."

"This one does," Julie said.

"Then you're lying."

"I'm not. There *is* a ghost. I saw it."

"Liar."

"I'm not!" She was screaming now. "I'll show you I'm not. I'll tell it to *get* you.

With its claws. It'll come and get you with its claws."

"Don't make me laugh."

"*Edward*! That's *enough*!" His mother stood up and started to clear the table. "Don't argue."

"But there isn't a ghost," Edward protested. "There can't be!"

Mrs Bennett glanced uneasily at Julie. "Of course there is," she said primly. "If Julie says so."

"She's a liar, a nasty little liar."

Julie kicked him hard, then, under the table. Edward yelped, and kicked back. Julie let out a screech, and then her face crumpled and she began to wail.

"*Now* look what you've done," Mrs Bennett snapped. "Oh *really*, Edward. You're twice her age. Why can't you leave her alone?"

"Because she's a liar, that's why." Edward stood up and pushed his chair aside. "Because there isn't a ghost in her bedroom. And even if there is, it won't have claws." He turned and stormed out of the kitchen.

He came to a stop in the sitting room, and crossed over to the window to see what sort of day it was going to be. Sunny, by the look of it. A small tightly-cropped lawn lay in front of the house, a lawn that was identical in size and appearance to those in front of the other identical square brick houses which lined the road. Edward laughed out loud. Any ghost worthy of the name would wither away from boredom in such surroundings. No, there weren't any ghosts in Briarfield Gardens. With or without heads under their arms. With or without claws.

He turned away from the window. The day had started badly, thanks to Julie. And it would continue badly, thanks to Julie and her rotten friends who were coming to tea. And there was nothing he could do about it. Or was there? On the coffee table by the television set there lay a half-finished jigsaw puzzle. Julie had been working on it for ages, her fair curls bent earnestly over the table day after day. According to the picture on the box, the finished puzzle would reveal a thatched cottage surrounded by a flower-filled garden. When it was finished. If.

Edward walked across to the table and smashed the puzzle with one quick, practised movement of his hand. Pieces fell and flew and scattered on the carpet in a storm of coloured cardboard. And then he turned, and ran upstairs to his room.

He hadn't long to wait. After a few minutes he heard the sounds that he was expecting. The kitchen door opening. A pause. Then a shrill, furious shriek, followed by loud sobbing. Running footsteps. A quieter comforting voice. Angry footsteps on the stairs. The rattling of the handle on his locked bedroom door. And then Julie's voice, not like a seven-year-old voice at all any more but harsh and bitter with hate.

"The ghost'll get you, Edward. I'm going to tell it to get you. With its claws. With its sharp, horrible claws."

And then, quite suddenly, Edward felt afraid.

The fear didn't last long. It had certainly

gone by lunchtime, when Edward was given a ticking-off by his father for upsetting dear little Julie. And by the time Julie's friends arrived at four, he was quite his old self again.

"The ugly sisters are here!" he announced loudly as he opened the front door, having beaten Julie to it by a short head.

She glared at him, and quickly hustled Sally and Rachel up the stairs to her room.

Edward felt a bit guilty. Sally and Rachel weren't at all ugly. In fact, he quite liked them both. He ambled into the kitchen, where his mother was busy preparing tea.

She looked up when he came in. "I do hope you're going to behave yourself this evening," she said. "We don't want a repetition of this morning's little episode, do we?"

"Well, she asked for it," Edward said sullenly, and sneaked a biscuit from a pile on a plate.

"Hands off!" his mother said automatically. "Julie did *not* ask for it. She was only pretending. You know what she's like. There was no need for you to be so nasty. And there was certainly no excuse for you to break up her jigsaw puzzle like that."

Edward shuffled uneasily and stared at the floor.

"She *is* only seven, after all," Mrs Bennett went on, slapping chocolate icing on a sponge cake as she did so. "You must make allowances. The rest of us do."

"She gets away with murder," Edward mumbled. "Just because she's such a sweet little girl."

"Nonsense!" his mother said firmly. "And keep your mucky paws off those ginger snaps. If anyone gets away with murder in this house, it's you."

"But she can't really expect us to believe there's a ghost in her bedroom," Edward said. "Do *you* believe her? Come on, Mum, do you?"

"I—" his mother began, and then she was interrupted by a familiar lisping voice.

"You *do* believe me, Mummy, don't you?"

Julie was standing at the kitchen door.

Edward wondered how long she'd been there. And how much she'd heard.

"Of course I do, darling," Mrs Bennett said quickly. "Now run along, both of you. Or I'll never have tea ready in time."

Julie stared at Edward for a moment with her cold blue eyes, and then she went out of the kitchen as quietly as she'd entered it.

Tea passed off smoothly enough. Julie seemed to be on her best behaviour but that was probably because her friends were there and she wanted to create a good impression. Edward followed her example. Julie didn't look at him or speak to him but there was nothing unusual about that. She and the others chattered brightly about nothing in particular, and Edward said nothing at all.

It was dusk by the time they'd finished tea and it was then that Julie suggested that they all play ghosts. She looked straight at Edward when she said this, and the proposal seemed like a challenge.

"Can anyone play?" he asked. "Or is it just a game for horrible little girls?"

"Edward!" warned his mother.

"Of course you can play, Edward," said Julie. "You *must* play."

"But not in the kitchen or in the dining room," said Mrs Bennett. "And keep out of our bedroom. I'll go and draw all the curtains and make sure the lights are switched off."

"All right," said Julie, and the other little girls clapped their hands with excitement.

"How do we play this stupid game?" said Edward.

"Oh, it's easy," said Julie. "One of us is the ghost, and she has to frighten the others. If the ghost catches you and scares you, you have to scream and drop down on the floor. As if you were dead."

"Like 'Murder in the Dark'?" asked Sally.

"Yes," said Julie. "Only we don't have a detective or anything like that."

"It sounds a crummy game to me," said Edward. "I don't think I'll play."

"Oh, *do*!" chorused Sally and Rachel. "Please!"

And Julie came up to him and whispered,

"You must play, Edward. And don't forget what I said this morning. About my ghost. And how it's going to get you with its claws."

"You must be joking!" Edward jeered. "And, anyway, I told you. Ghosts don't have claws." He looked her straight in the eyes. "Of course I'll play."

Julie smiled, and then turned to the others and said, "I'll be the ghost to start with. The rest of you run and hide. I'll count up to fifty and then I'll come and haunt you."

Sally and Rachel galloped upstairs, squealing with excitement. Edward wandered into the hall and stood for a moment, wondering where to hide. It wasn't going to be easy. Their small brick box of a house didn't offer many possibilities. After a while he decided on the sitting room. It was the most obvious place and Julie would never think of looking there. He opened the door quietly, ducked down behind an armchair, and waited.

Silence settled over the house. Apart from washing-up sounds from the kitchen, all was quiet. Edward made himself comfortable on the carpet and waited for the distant screams that would tell him that Sally had been discovered, or Rachel. But no sounds came. As he waited, ears straining against the silence, the room grew darker. The day was fading and it would soon be night.

And then, suddenly, Edward heard a slight noise near the door. His heart leapt and, for some reason, his mouth went dry. And then the fear returned, the unaccountable fear he had felt that morning when Julie hissed her threat through his bedroom door.

The air seemed much colder now, but that could only be his imagination, surely. But he knew that he wasn't imagining the wild thumping of his heart or the sickening lurching of his stomach. He remembered Julie's words and swallowed hard.

"The ghost'll get you, Edward. With its claws. With its sharp, horrible claws."

He heard sounds again, closer this time. A scuffle. Whispering. Or was it whispering? Someone was there. Something. He tried to speak, but gave only a curious croak. And then, "Julie?" he said. "I know you're there. I know it's you."

Silence. A dark terrible silence. And then the light snapped on and the room was filled with laughter and shouts of "Got you! Caught you! The ghost has caught you!", and he saw Julie's face alive with triumph and delight, and, behind her, Sally and Rachel grinning, and the fear was replaced by an anger far darker and more intense than the terror he'd felt before.

"Edward's scared of the ghost!" Julie jeered. "Edward's a scaredy cat! He's frightened! He's frightened of the ghost!"

And Rachel and Sally echoed her. "He's frightened! He's frightened of the ghoost!"

"I'm not!" Edward shouted. "I'm not scared! There isn't a ghost!" And he pushed past Julie and ran out of the room and up the stairs. He'd show her. He'd prove she didn't have a ghost. There were no such things as ghosts. She didn't have a ghost in her room. She didn't.

Julie's bedroom was empty. Apart from

the furniture and the pictures and the toys and dolls and knick-knacks. He opened the wardrobe and pulled shoes and games out on to the floor. He burrowed in drawers, scattering books and stuffed animals and clothes around him. At last he stopped, gasping for breath. And turned.

His mother was standing in the doorway, staring at him in amazement. Clustered behind her were the puzzled, anxious faces of Sally and Rachel. And behind them, Julie. Looking at him with her ice-blue eyes.

"What on earth are you doing?" his mother asked.

"See?" he panted. "There isn't a ghost here. She hasn't got a ghost in her bedroom. There's nothing here. Nothing."

"Isn't there?" said Julie. "Are you sure you've looked properly?"

Sally – or was it Rachel? – gave a nervous giggle.

"That's enough," said Mrs Bennett. "Now I suggest you tidy up the mess you've made in here, Edward, and then go to your room. I don't know why you're

behaving so strangely. But it's got to stop. It's got to."

She turned and went downstairs. Sally and Rachel followed her. Julie lingered by the door, and stared mockingly at Edward. He stared back.

"It's still here, you know," she said at last. "The ghost is still here. And it'll get you."

"You're a dirty little liar!" he shouted. "A nasty, filthy little liar!"

Julie gaped at him for a moment, taken aback by the force of his rage. Then, "It'll get you!" she screamed. "With its claws. Its horrible claws. It'll get you tonight. When you're asleep. Because I hate you. I hate you. Yes, it'll *really* get you. Tonight."

It was dark when Edward awoke. At first he didn't know where he was. And then he remembered. He was in bed. In his bedroom. It was the middle of the night. And he remembered, too, Julie's twisted face and the things she said. The face and the words had kept him awake, and had haunted his dreams when at last he slept.

It was ridiculous, really. All this fuss about an imaginary ghost. Why did he get in such a state over Julie? She was only a little kid, after all. His baby sister. You were supposed to love your sister, not – not fear her. But no, he wasn't *really* afraid of her. How could he be? Such a sweet little girl with blue eyes and fair bouncing curls who was half his age. A little girl who played games and imagined things. Who imagined ghosts. A ghost in her bedroom.

But he *was* frightened. He knew that now. And as his fear mounted again, the room seemed to get colder. He shut his eyes and snuggled down under the blankets, shutting out the room and the cold. But not the fear.

And then he heard it. A sound. A faint scraping sound, as though something heavy was being dragged along the landing. A sound that came closer and grew louder. A wet, slithering sound. And with it came a smell, a sickening smell of, oh, drains and dead leaves and decay. And the sound grew louder and he could hear breathing, harsh breathing, long choking breaths coming closer.

"Julie?" Edward said, and then he repeated it, louder. "Julie!"

But there was no answer. All he heard was the scraping, dragging sound coming closer, closer. Near his door now. Closer.

"I know it's you!" Edward shouted, and heard the fear in his voice. "You're playing ghosts again, aren't you? Aren't you?"

And then there was silence. No sound at all. Edward sat up in bed and listened. The awful slithering noise had stopped. It had gone. The ghost had gone.

He hugged himself with relief. It had been a dream, that's all. He'd imagined it. Just as Julie imagined things. Imagined ghosts.

Then he heard the breathing again. The shuddering, choking breaths. And he knew that the thing hadn't gone. That it was still there. Outside his door. Waiting. Waiting.

And Edward screamed, "Julie! Stop it! Stop it! Please stop it! I believe you! I believe in the ghost!"

The door opened. The shuddering breaths

seemed to fill the room, and the smell, and the slithering wet sound of a shape, something, coming towards him, something huge and dark and—

And he screamed as the claws, yes, the claws tore at his hands, his chest, his face. And he screamed again as the darkness folded over him.

When Julie woke up and came downstairs, the ambulance had gone. Her mother was sitting alone in the kitchen, looking pale and frightened. She smiled weakly when she saw Julie, and then frowned.

"Darling," she said. "I did so hope you wouldn't wake up. I didn't want you to be frightened—"

"What's the matter, Mummy?" said Julie. "Why are you crying?"

Her mother smiled again, and drew Julie to her, folding her arms round her so that she was warm and safe. "You must be very brave, darling," she said. "Poor Edward has been hurt. We don't know what happened but he's been very badly hurt."

"Hurt? What do you mean, Mummy?"

Her mother brushed a stray curl from the little girl's face. "We don't know what happened, exactly. Something attacked him. His face—" Her voice broke then, and she looked away quickly. "He has been very badly scratched. They're not sure if his eyes—" She stopped and fumbled in her dressing-gown pocket for a tissue.

"I expect my ghost did it," Julie said smugly.

"What did you say, dear?"

Julie looked up at her mother. "My ghost did it. I told it to. I told it to hurt Edward because I hate him. The ghost hurt him. The ghost in my bedroom."

Mrs Bennett stared at Julie. "This is no time for games," she said. "We're very upset. Your father's gone to the hospital with Edward. We don't know if—" Her eyes filled with tears. "I'm in no mood for your silly stories about ghosts, Julie. Not now. I'm too upset."

"But it's true!" Julie said. "My ghost *did* do it. Because I told it to."

Mrs Bennett pushed her away and stood up. "All right, Julie, that's enough. Back to bed now. You can play your game tomorrow."

"But it's not a game," Julie persisted. "It's true! My ghost—"

And then she saw the angry expression on her mother's face, and she stopped. Instead, she snuggled up to her and whispered, "I'm sorry, Mummy. You're right. I *was* pretending. I was only pretending about the ghost. There isn't a ghost in my room. I was making it all up. And I'm so sorry about poor Edward."

Mrs Bennett relaxed and smiled and drew Julie to her once more. "That's my baby," she said softly. "That's my sweet little girl. Of course you were only pretending. Of course there wasn't a ghost. Would I let a nasty ghost come and frighten my little girl? Would I? Would I?"

"No, Mummy," said Julie. "Of course you wouldn't."

"Off you go to bed now."

"Good night, Mummy," said Julie.

"Sleep well, my pet," said her mother.

And Julie walked out of the kitchen and into the hall and up the stairs to her bedroom. She went inside and closed the door behind her.

And the ghost came out to meet her.

"She doesn't believe me, either," Julie said. "She doesn't believe me. We'll have to show her, won't we? Just as we showed Edward."

And the ghost smiled and nodded, and they sat down together, Julie and the ghost, and decided what they would do.

Storm Children

PAULINE HILL

I'm not one to swank, but I reckon I'm pretty good at lots of things. Not sums and spelling and Scottish dancing (my legs go wrong in the twisty bits) ... but, well, scrambling eggs for instance, and sewing the hem of my sister's dress when it comes undone (as it does most times she comes home after chasing in the field with the Baker kids, they always find the filthiest places to skip and slide in). What's more, I'm always first up the ropes in the gym, and I finish first with my paper-round, if old Mrs Hennessey doesn't pop out in her red dressing-gown for a yarn.

There's no end to the things I *can* do. Sometimes when I feel sulky, I'll hunt out the posh writing-pad Aunt Cynthia gave me for Christmas and my red felt-tip, the one that I keep for recording Riotous Events, and make a list of everything I *can* do, just to cheer myself up. Loads of things.

1 *I'm the only one on our street who's actually grown hollyhocks*
2 *And great big sunflowers so that I can feed Mrs Pankhurst's hens with the seeds, and Mrs Pankhurst sometimes gives me new-laid eggs, so that's a bonus*
3 *And I'm always the first to find snowdrops in the woods*
4 *And violets*
5 *And last autumn I made ten jars of blackberry jam from blackberries I picked in the woods*
6 *And I brush my dog Shaggy's coat till it*

*glistens like spun silk, and he won 1st prize
at the Dog Show*
7 *And some kids haven't even got dogs they
can take for walks in the fields and go
down to the market to buy biscuits for*

But there's one thing that always really frightened me. More than ghosts. More than witches. More than little green men from Outer Space. I didn't tell anyone about it, because looking at me you wouldn't think I was frightened of anything, ever. But I couldn't get through a thunderstorm without shivering and trembling and getting in a right old tizz. Once I even wet my pants, I was so scared. But I kept the fear to myself mostly. It's better not to tell folks what you're afraid of, they find out soon enough.

It really was strange how I came to be cured of thunderstorms. Part of it's to do with Mr Trenchard, my history teacher. He's mad on old buildings, monuments, old crumbly houses and spooky castles. Once he took our class to peer at a Roman Wall,

all broken away and powdery with beetles crawling all over, I didn't think much of it. My dad builds much better walls. I could've summoned up a faint glimmer of excitement if we'd actually seen Roman soldiers building it, but when I mentioned it to Mr Trenchard he seemed a bit put out. "Don't be stupid, Tracey. Try to use the few brains you've got, child!" Which was a bit off. I can't stand grown-ups who call me "child."

We had to do one of those questionnaires about the Roman Wall. I got all the answers from Peter Green. My marks were quite high in that questionnaire, it certainly surprised Mr Trenchard. But I did like the stories he told us about our town in wartime. My mum won't ever tell me about the War, she says it's better forgotten; but Mr Trenchard keeps bits of old planes in his garage, and lets kids polish them, and he'll sometimes give out Mars Bars too. He's got a photo of himself in RAF uniform when he was a pilot in the Battle of Britain, he looked quite handsome in those days. One September night in 1940 his squadron shot down an enemy plane over Devil's Finger, just a few miles away. The pilot baled out, over the woods, but his parachute got caught in the branches of a tree, and he was killed.

Well, this year, we had a half-day holiday in September because the vicar said we'd worked so hard bringing in the stuff for Harvest Festival (HP Sauce and conkers was what soppy Jenkins offered) and he wanted us to enjoy the warm weather before winter set in. Shaggy was waiting when I got home after school dinner – mince and salad, I ask you – and we set off towards the woods.

Lots of deep blue sky, bright golden sunshine on the stubble fields, and Shaggy belting off after imaginary rabbits in the hedgerows. I love walking. Shaggy likes walking too. I've never known a dog who doesn't. So we must have gone four or five miles, and I hardly noticed the candy-floss clouds slipping off the edge of the sky.

But, stealthily, grey shadows crept up. I felt a plop of warm rain on my arm. And then . . . CRACK! A heavy rumble.

Fields lately friendly with sunshine became eerie, sinister. A flurry of wind lifted the leaves under the trees. Shaggy slunk close to me, tail between his legs, and licked my hand. "It's all right, boy," I comforted him, knowing that he was scared too. A dagger of lightning knifed across the sky. Thunder boomed overhead . . . rain cut down in solid sheets. Terror gripped me . . . sheer blind panic! I must get away . . . anywhere, away from it all . . . Stumbling wildly, I ran on through the trees . . .

I came upon the farmhouse suddenly. *Acres Bottom Farm* it said on the gate. One minute it wasn't there . . . the next it was.

I knew Mum wouldn't approve of me going up to a strange house, but I was so scared that I peered in at the window, and saw a big farm kitchen, with a wide and welcoming log fire roaring up the chimney – in September – and children, four, five, six of them, dancing in the firelight. I banged on the door, the children came rushing to open it, and a moment later Shaggy and I were inside the warm kitchen. It smelt apple-sweet and spicy with cinnamon. Rosy-cheeked, smiling, chattering like magpies, the children danced and clapped their hands. "You found us. We knew you would!" said the tallest boy. "We've been waiting so long." They grabbed both my hands and pulled me into their frantic dance. They barely heard the claps of thunder, but I could see flashes of lightning through the windows. "Don't you *love* storms?" asked one little girl.

"No . . . no. I don't."

"But you *must!*" she cried. "They're beautiful!"

Another deafening clap of thunder. The children laughed and laughed, dancing more furiously, forcing me to join in . . . making me dance and squeal and fight back against the storm with yells and laughs and dancing, dancing, dancing.

I don't know how long the storm lasted. It was over too soon for me. The fear inside me suddenly snapped, and I'd never felt so wild and happy as I did that afternoon with the Storm Children.

It was well into evening, a calm and pastel sky after the fury. "I must go now."

"Promise to come again! Promise!"

"I will! I will!"

Mum had seen the gathering black clouds earlier, and had feared for me. She was on the afternoon shift at the clothing factory that week. When the storm broke she phoned Dad. He wasn't pleased. He was working nights, and hated being woken early, but Mum can be very persuasive. He uttered a few ripe words under his breath and went out looking for me. He hunted high and low, asked each soul he met . . . but returned home alone.

Mum panicked, of course, and he got the sharp end of her tongue. She'd come home early from the factory – she does fuss a lot. She rounded on him fiercely, demanding, "Haven't you found her?" She always tosses her head haughtily when she's mad at Dad. Dad says it's her "High Dudgeon" mood.

So when I'd said goodbye to the Storm kids in the warm house and promised to come back with some blackberry jam for them to taste, I ran home to find Mum in a High Dudgeon. "Well!" she glared crossly when I came in. "A fine dance you've led us, young lady!"

"Hello, Mum."

"Dad's been out looking for you! Where've you been, you naughty girl?"

"I sheltered in a house. When the storm came on. You know . . ."

"Of course I know how frightened you get. I used to be just the same! Which house was it? I've told you not to go into strange houses . . . not to talk to strangers . . ." She was white with anger. Dad says though she gets angry her heart's in the right place.

"Oh, Mum," I said, and gave her a hug.

"Which house?" Her tone softened. "Which house, Tracey?"

"A farmhouse up near Devil's Finger."

She didn't reply immediately. Then she said, "There's no farmhouse up at Devil's Finger." She looked sharply at Dad. "Is there, Tom?"

"Well . . ." He picked up Mum's warning

look. "No. No farmhouse. There *used* to be . . ."

"You must know it," I said. "It's a farm called Acres Bottom. Funny name, isn't it? Mum . . . you all right?" She'd turned so pale that I thought she was going to faint.

"I feel . . . a bit giddy," she said. "You know how I get."

After, when Mum had popped round next door to see Mrs Pankhurst, Dad said, "Your mum's always been nervy, love. Ever since I first knew her. She was only your age, then. She still gets frightened sometimes."

"By thunderstorms?"

"She's better than she used to be. But she gets jumpy about all sorts of things."

"That place. Acres Bottom . . ."

"There used to be a farm by that name. Back in the War: 1940, it must have been – bombing every blessed night. An enemy plane was shot down near Devil's Finger. It crashed on the farmhouse. Terrible disaster . . . all six kids killed in their beds."

I gasped.

Dad went on, "They say Acres Wood's

haunted by the ghost of the German pilot. People reckon they've seen him on September evenings. All nonsense, of course, but you know how your mum gets."

When Mum came back from next door, everything seemed different. I had suddenly grown older. I knew two things. I would never again be afraid of thunderstorms. And I knew that when I was Mum's age, I should never be afraid of things that still frightened her.

Months later, Mum asked casually, though her hands were clenched as she spoke, "That day of the thunderstorm, Tracey. When you were in the woods that evening . . .you didn't see anything . . .?"

I laughed gently. "Oh, Mum," I said. "You've been listening to those silly stories about the ghost of the German pilot."

"Well . . .?"

"Of course not. That's all nonsense!"

But I never told her what I *had* seen, at Acres Bottom.

Blondin's Rainbow

Judith Vidal

There was once a man called Blondin. He
could walk higher and finer than any man
in the world. So high and fine was his
walking that he thought he would try the
most difficult walk ever made, the highest
and finest of any man. A wire was stretched
tight and high, and a thousand feet long,
above the waters of Niagara in the USA,
the highest, deepest waterfall in the world.
Blondin walks again!

For it was not the first time that Blondin

had come to Niagara. He had been here before. He had done all that it was possible to do. He had wheeled wheelbarrows on his wire across the Falls; carried men on his back – men who trusted him; blind-folded without his eyes; on stilts that rocked as he walked. And finally, his most spectacular achievement of all, he had made and eaten an omelette there in the middle of his wire. He had carried his eggs and eaten them all. The crowds had gone wild with the joy and suspense.

And now here he was again. The hopes of the crowd were high, though their imagination failed. "What would it be this time?" they asked themselves. "What could he do that he had not already done?" Standing excitedly in the thin drizzle which had begun to fall they watched the arrival of the great man. "A little older," they said. "A bit too old, perhaps, for this sort of thing. You have to know when to stop: quit whilst there's still time." They shook their heads quietly, and raised quizzical eyebrows. Many of them were privately certain that he

would not make it this time. He was fatter,
more bulging in the calf, and his famous
twirled moustache looked a little sad. But
maybe he had learned a new trick or two,
and they looked forward to some new and
dazzling feat about to be performed above
their heads, never believing for one minute
that the wire alone could be enough, be it as
high as never was. That, they thought, would
be a cheat and disappointment. They hadn't
travelled all those miles in the rain and early
morning just for that. But they needn't worry
they decided. This was Blondin. And they
cheered him as he stepped amongst them.

Indeed, all over Europe they had not
ceased to cheer him. In circus rings, as
high over the sawdust as it was possible to
be, the lights above dazzling the eyes of those
below, they had lifted up their faces to watch
him, silent and intent. No one breathed. The
children, or some of them, shut their eyes
as he started out. Some stuffed their fists,
tightly clenched, into their mouths to hold
down a scream that might leak out. Others
pushed their longest finger into each ear to

keep out the crash. But there was never a crash. Every time the breathing which had stopped started again in a great sigh which rippled round the ring. The eyes opened, the fists and fingers came out to clap, and the new found voices cheered for all they were worth. "Blondin! Blondin!"

They came from miles to see him in fairgrounds, circuses, music-halls. His name was in the brightest lights: he headed every bill. But still, it seemed, for him it was not enough. "I must get higher; stretch the wire finer." He was never satisfied. He out-topped the biggest Big Top, and walked on his wire in the highest buildings men could offer. He even performed in magical palaces of glass over the heads of royalty, turned somersaults over them in air in the soaring glass cage. Steadily and elegantly he walked and performed. His precarious balance looked like security to those who watched from below. They marvelled, and praised him all over the world. His life history appeared in the newspapers. They made up songs about him and sold them on the streets. And so he had finally come to Niagara to dance for them on his wire; to amaze and startle them with his tricks.

Now here he was again. Niagara he had crossed the Ocean to walk once more. He had to do it though he didn't exactly know why. It wasn't that he particularly wanted to any more, because it was true that he was old and tired now – perhaps was losing his skill. But it was there, and would remain there as long as he could put one foot forward on to a tight-rope. And this one time now, with the wire at its new and impossibly dizzy height, was the most important moment in his life. This time was different from all the occasions in the past. Only Blondin knew. There would be no tricks this time. He was done with crowds. The cheers no longer mattered. He'd had those all his life as long as he could remember. This time there was just Blondin and his wire, higher than ever before, higher than even he had imagined. The waters seemed further and deeper than he had ever known, yet so near, and for almost the first time in his life, so easy to fall into. He looked at the wire and was afraid. The terrible drop between the wire and the deeps below was a gap he could feel. Never had he thought to know this within himself. Others had spoken of it before climbing to their wires and trapezes, but not Blondin.

As he looked, his past triumphs seemed to melt away. Nothing he'd done before mattered any longer, and to make things worse, he no longer knew if he could make it across his wire this time. He thought about the things he might do instead. Change his act altogether, perhaps, or just stop, give up, retire, unsurpassed in the eyes of the world. He'd earned a rest, and he'd made enough money in his performing life to live comfortably for the rest of it. But somehow he couldn't do that yet. This was the only real thing left to him, and he just had to get across for the last time. It wasn't simply that the wire was higher than ever before, nor that the Falls seemed so impossibly long down. He had to conquer the gap that filled his mind and made him tremble, so that his knees wouldn't stop jumping of their own accord, and his toes twitched on the red carpet with which they had paved his way to the wire.

The crowd had grown bigger than ever. Someone had spread the story that this was to be the last time: Blondin's swan-song. He'd never perform again, whether he crossed the wire or not. They whispered that it was all or nothing with him, and waited impatiently for something to happen. They had come from all over the countryside, people who had heard of this man, had not believed, had laughed incredulously, and now had come to see for themselves. Most of them had never set foot on a wire, had never climbed higher than the fencing which surrounded their chicken-runs at home. But there were, too, those who had dreamed of the high-wire in moments of time, and who regretted never having tested its strength with their own. They had come to see and experience at secondhand the thrills they had missed. There were the sceptics who had come to see him fall; the simple who came to be entertained. Finally there were the old "Pros", his brothers in the art, who had walked the tightrope themselves, and now had come to watch with wise eyes the performance of their acknowledged master. These were the ones who walked the wire with him, who knew the taste in his mouth and the tightness of his throat. They would have held his hands and helped him over if they could, but they knew the aloneness, that it could be no other than it was. Besides, this was higher than any of them had ever reached; they had retired before Niagara.

Blondin walked up to where the thin silver wire stretched away from him over the emptiness beneath and the deeps below. Then he walked on further along the cliff top to look over into this great abyss. He saw the boiling crashing waters far, far below him. They thrashed and beat on the tumbled rocks at the bottom, and broke into white foaming fragments. Everything was confused and half-hidden by the glittering spray which shot back up from the shattering.

The crowd gasped. How could he bear

to look? Everybody knew that heights were all right as long as you never looked down. It wasn't good to know how steep the drop, how terrible the fall, the crash at the bottom. It was better to keep your eyes fixed ahead, to look up even. Only then could you keep your mind empty of the drop. Not to know what lay beneath was the only possible way to succeed.

But Blondin knew what waited for him down there. He had seen it before, though never so clearly as now – and it had filled his mind for years. Now he leaned far out over the edge to stare, only confirming what he had always known. The broken rocks and crashing water, the steep drop through emptiness, the gap between here and there, were more real in his mind than in his eyes as he looked.

He got up from where he had been hanging over the edge. Better get on with it. He felt a little stiff from the wetness of the air around him, and his knees cracked from the cold damp of the earth. It wasn't a good day. Indeed his manager, on arriving at the site, had strongly urged him not to attempt the crossing that day; to come back tomorrow, the next day, any day – so long as it was calm and still. But for Blondin it was the only day. As he waited he knew that the time had come. This was the right day for him, and he couldn't wait any longer.

He was not unduly troubled by the clouds that hung low and grey in the sky, nor by the coldness in his joints. A thin mist had gathered above the Falls, and in the middle swallowed up the wire so that it seemed not to be there. The thin wire, stretched so tight and high, reached out into nothingness: stopped in mid-air. He could see no end, and it seemed too, that to walk into invisibility might result in his stepping into the gap. "Don't go. Don't go," his manager urged. "Of course, it's a pity to disappoint the crowd, but they'll come back. They always do. Anything for a thrill." Privately, the crowd was thinking not of the walk, but of a fall. They felt a strange tension as the thought of tragedy touched them. They became restless with suppressed excitement and anticipation. Now they were urging a decision one way or the other. Some, like the manager, urged prudence, another day. Others, unwilling to be cheated of the spectacle, shouted at Blondin to "Get on with it!"

The manager, wrapped up fatly in his great coat with the tight belt and fur collar, so enveloped he could scarcely move his arms, felt strongly about risking his prize exhibit. This was his livelihood after all, and had he not the right to grow fatter yet on Blondin's back? Yet still Blondin knew. Here was now, and he must go over or never. It worried him a little that the wire disappeared, that the opposite cliff was invisible. Worse still was the wind. It wasn't felt all the time, but blew spasmodically in sharp gusts which opened coats and snatched hats. It could be nasty, he thought, to meet that halfway across. It could upset the poise, whip up the ends of his pole on which he relied so strongly to retain his balance. The pole itself could become a danger. Still, he knew the wire was there, had seen it glinting in the sun the day before, thin and fine, but securely fixed and there all the way over. Now it hummed slightly, and sang into the wind. He felt a deep fondness for his wire warming him. He longed to be nothing else than he was. He would go. Nobody should stop him. The crowd was unimportant. He was alone. Blondin and his wire. The chaotic waters beneath, most of all that long gap, were his. Not even the thought of his manager, anxiously puffing out clouds of steam and stamping his feet, could make any difference. He liked him well enough. Jolly fellow, and a great help on the business side, the organisation, the money. He'd set the whole thing up out there. But well – he wasn't walking. It wasn't his wire.

Blondin stretched out his hand for the pole that would help him in his walk. It was thin and long and undulating as he grasped it firmly in both hands stretched out before him. He was ready to walk. He set his foot on the wire, bouncing it up and down to get the mood of it, to accustom his feet to its familiar feel. It was all right: firm, tense, and there all the way. The crowd was disappointed he didn't turn and wave. They would have liked to cheer. Poor showmanship. Things like that looked bad in a public performer. They did not know, how could they, that for Blondin they simply were not there. He had begun what he came for. Now there was only the wire, the broken deep below, the space between – together with the cold wind inside. He must reach the other side, and he would.

He took his first step forward. The wire began to move and sway beneath him as it always did. He was used to that. He bobbed and balanced as he stood there. The wind still troubled him. A cold eddy took the ends of the pole and whipped them up and down in its breath. Dangerous. Better to be rid of it now than be clinging on at the wrong moment. The pole fell silently, slowly, swiftly down. There was an exclamation from the crowd. The fat manager let out a strangled scream which was lost in the thunder of the waters. Blondin didn't hear. He felt better without the pole. Now it was really just him. He would do better than he thought: be more alone than he had imagined. He stretched out his arms rigidly on each side, looked straight and firm across to the invisible other side, and slowly at first, then almost trippingly, set out.

His feet slid their way along the wire, smoothly feeling out their path. He was light and could have danced. It didn't matter, he told himself, that he couldn't see the wire further on. His feet could feel it and that was all that mattered. In any case, maybe the mist would clear before he got there. It might not even cover much of the wire, and he would soon be through. He went on forward.

Now he was approaching the mist. His feet continued, but the grey folds were cold and wet. It was a sheet thrown over his head to confuse and hamper his movements. Yet still he was all right. He knew his wire and trusted his feet. His arms swayed each side of him like twin vanes. But now the wire began to twitch and sway treacherously. A wind inside the fog swirled it around

him, hanging damp obscure folds over him,
baffling his senses as it closed tighter on him.
He couldn't go on. The wind and fog were
too strong against him. Into his mind came
the thought of turning back whilst he still
could. Perhaps it would be wiser after all. No
one would blame him under conditions like
these. They'd even cheer, probably. "Never
mind, Blondin, you'll do it yet." He saw the
droop of his moustache as he stepped on to
firm land, felt the shame in his eyes. The
crowd parted to let him through, comforting
him as he passed. Their respect for his
earlier triumphs would be unimpaired. For
Blondin it was the feeling of defeat. It was
there, then gone. Blondin felt no more. He
knew there was no going back. To turn in
the fog and wind was impossible.

His mind was a stone. His feet were
numb and unfeeling on the wire. It was
dark, and he couldn't go forward. He
twitched and swayed with the wire in the
effort to retain his precarious balance. Only
that unfelt determination kept him upright.
Not even the long gap was in his mind,

though somewhere deep was the knowledge that if he had to fall he would. Better that than go back. Blondin stood and waited. He was high over nothing, hidden by fog in the middle of his wire. In his mind he was in the water below, broken on the rocks. He had fallen through the gap.

On the side from which he had started the crowd had watched him disappear. A few drifted away, knowing they would not see him arrive at the other side. They were cold for their homes and firesides. The rest remained, waiting around for something they didn't know what. Though the far cliff was invisible, someone, they were sure, would send word what had happened. Maybe the cheers would echo back from the other side. In any case, you couldn't just leave someone out on a limb like that. No, better stay and see.

On the far side the expectant unknowing crowd stared hard with reddening eyes and cold hands. They tried to peer into the heart of the fog, hoping to see a small wraith emerging towards them. They strained to see, and it seemed a long time. There was nothing there yet. They looked at watches and knew that it was taking too long. It was getting late. Either he hadn't started (and you couldn't blame him really; it was a foul day), or . . . Just then the message filtered through that Blondin was on his way. They stretched their eyes further into the swirling fog which seemed at moments to part, only to come together again more impenetrably than before. There was nothing there. The wind was trying, perhaps, to blow away the clouds, but it would certainly blow away Blondin too, if it hadn't already.

The long silent minutes ticked by. They began to be afraid: to fear for Blondin, that something had happened to him. He couldn't come now. No one, not even the Maestro, could hang that long in air. It was all over. Yet they hadn't heard a cry. Maybe the wind had blown it back to the other side, or the noise of the waters drowned it. The fear that the worst had happened grew. No eyes met, though they no longer looked out from their end of the wire. The crowd was restless. They didn't know what to do. No one spoke, except the children who still expected the great man to appear at any moment and couldn't understand why there were tears in the grown-up eyes. "When's he coming, Papa?" "Mama, where is he?" "Come on Blondin!" "We want Blondin!" Their parents hushed them from above. It was all a bit puzzling. Perhaps he wasn't coming today after all. Perhaps he'd turned back. They hoped not, because they loved Blondin, the pictures and photographs they had seen of the funny little man. Well, it was hard luck, but he'd come some day they believed. Even if it could not be Blondin there were other men with wires and poles. They, better than the grown-ups, knew the problems. For hadn't they, many of them, practised on the wire fences around the place? They'd had some bangs and bruises, even broken arms and legs, at which their parents had drawn the line and forbidden such dangerous games. Still there were a few who secretly went on practising, and could not give up until the day when they too would be walking over Niagara. But the parents knew that Blondin had fallen, had failed, was by now dead. And they could not bring themselves to tell their children.

Blondin on the wire stood. And he stood, and he stood. And the cold stone in his mind sank as the wind parted the fog and whipped up the cold folds from his shoulders. A thin silver thread stretched once more in front of him. His feet began to move forward of their own accord, lightly and calmly. Blondin, arms straight out, head high, walked forward again, unseeing to the other side.

The crowd who had stopped looking, who despaired, saw a grey shadow. It couldn't be! It was! No! It wasn't possible! He must have gone down by this time! – But yes! It was, it really was! He was coming! He was through! A great cheer began, but was broken before it hit the air. He hadn't actually arrived yet, had he? Plenty could happen between here and there. Many a slip and all. The slightest mistake at any moment on the wire slippery with wetness, and the wind even stronger now, could cause disaster. But he was coming – and fast too. Heavens, the man was mad! He was actually running! He wasn't down. Here he came. There was a gasp of horror as his arms swirled wildly. He was nearly with them now. He was going to do it. They couldn't believe it, but were immeasurably glad. Hands reached out ready to grasp him. He'd made it. He'd arrived. He was here.

A great cheer, unchecked this time, welcomed him. "Blondin! Blondin! Hurrah! Hurrah!" And Blondin, cold and wet from the water which had splashed him, and the dampness which had soaked beneath his skin, stood weary and exhausted on land again. Firm wet brown and green land stretched either side of the second red carpet. He'd done it. He looked back. The mist had lifted, blown up on the wind. The thin silver line stretched all the way back to the other side. He could see the crowd there leaping and waving – cheering too, no doubt. Blondin smiled. He smiled a smile that was weary, but happy and wise too, because he'd crossed the tight-rope, and knew that never again would he have to fall into the abyss, the waters.

As he looked he saw what he had never seen before, the bridge that spanned the waterfall. It shone and glowed in all its colours. The spray glittered and was transformed in the light. It arced over the churning below, complete from side to side. Curious. It was always there. He'd just never noticed it before.

Acknowledgements

Anita Desai and Rogers, Coleridge & White Ltd for 'Secrets' from *Guardian Angels* (Viking Kestrel, 1987), © Anita Desai 1987. Adele Geras & Laura Cecil Literary Agency for 'Wordfinder', © Adele Geras 1987. Charles Mungoshi and Baobab Books for 'The Slave who became Chief', from *Stories from a Shona Childhood*. Susan Shrieve and Russell & Volkening Inc for 'Cheating', from *Family Secrets*. Ann Pilling and Gina Pollinger for 'The Old Stone Faces' from *Mists and Magic* ed. Dorothy Edwards (Lutterworth/Fonatana, 1983). Sally Christie for 'Fishing with Dicky'. Alexander McCall Smith and Canongate Publishing Ltd for 'Children of Wax' from *Children of Wax* (Canongate, 1987). Ted Hughes and Faber & Faber Ltd for 'The Snag' from *Tales of the Early World*, published by Faber & Faber Ltd. Robin Klein and Haytul Pty Ltd c/o Curtis Brown (Aust Pty Ltd, Sydney) for 'Hey, Danny!' from *Ratbags and Rascals*. Michael Rosen and the English & Media Centre for 'The Bakerloo Flea' from *Teachers' Writing*. Jan Mark and Penguin Books Ltd for 'Marrow Hill' from *Nothing to be Afraid Of* (Kestrel Books, 1980). Lance Salway and Rogers, Coleridge & White Ltd for 'Such a Sweet Little Girl' from *A Nasty Piece of Work* (John Murray, 1988). Pauline Hill for 'Storm Children' from *Mists and Magic* (Lutterworth/Fonatana, 1983). Judith Vidal and Macmillan Publishers Ltd for 'Blondin's Rainbow' from *Young Writers' Tales 3* ed. M R Hodgkin (1972).

The publishers gratefully acknowledge the above for permission to reproduce copyright material. Whilst every effort has been made to trace the appropriate sources for the stories in this collection, in the event of an erroneous credit the publishers will be more than happy to make corrections in any reprint editions.

239